A Candlelight
Ecstasy Romance ®

## "AREN'T YOU A LITTLE OLD
## TO BE DEALING IN FANTASIES?"
## KASHA ASKED BLUNTLY.

Jeff straightened in his chair and grinned at her. "You're real, aren't you?"

Her voice was dry, decisive. "Yes, I'm real. But that has absolutely nothing to do with the fact that you're deluding yourself. I can tell you now in clear terms that I will never become involved with you. And I can't help you. You definitely need help, but not from me."

Conscious that he was rising, she stopped speaking. It all happened so fast, she couldn't be sure how it had happened. Suddenly she was looking at him wildly and he was holding her in his arms.

"You know, Kasha," he whispered. "I have the suspicion that somewhere beneath that big white coat beats a warm and tender heart. And that's all I want—your heart."

## A CANDLELIGHT ECSTASY ROMANCE ®

# A
# CLASSIC
# LOVE

*Jo Calloway*

*A CANDLELIGHT ECSTASY ROMANCE* ®

Published by
Dell Publishing Co., Inc.
1 Dag Hammarskjold Plaza
New York, New York 10017

ISBN: 0-440-11242-7

Printed in the United States of America
First printing—March 1984

To Our Readers:

We have been delighted with your enthusiastic response to Candlelight Ecstasy Romances®, and we thank you for the interest you have shown in this exciting series.

In the upcoming months we will continue to present the distinctive sensuous love stories you have come to expect only from Ecstasy. We look forward to bringing you many more books from your favorite authors and also the very finest work from new authors of contemporary romantic fiction.

As always, we are striving to present the unique, absorbing love stories that you enjoy most—books that are more than ordinary romance.

Your suggestions and comments are always welcome. Please write to us at the address below.

Sincerely,

The Editors
Candlelight Romances
1 Dag Hammarskjold Plaza
New York, New York 10017

# CHAPTER ONE

Jeff Bannerman took a bite of hot dog and chewed vigorously a moment, then lifted the opened carton of milk to his mouth and emptied it. Raising his arm, he wiped his lips on the sleeve of his gray twill shirt, then placed the rest of the hot dog in his mouth, his eyes not moving an inch from the front entrance of the Orman Building. Swallowing, he glanced briefly at his digital watch, then back to the building entrance. Twelve-five. If she was true to schedule today, he knew it was time for her to emerge for lunch.

The bright Florida sun shone down through a cloudless June sky and bounced off the bright yellow hardhat pushed back on his head. He watched the doorway, his eyes narrowing in anticipation. The seconds ticked by and he scanned the face of his watch, then concentrated again on the building across the street. Suddenly he frowned. Twelve-seven. She was late—most unusual for her. Until today he could have set his watch by her promptness. Impatience tugged at him and he stood slowly, straightening his tall, slender muscular body to his full height of six two, shaking his head with just the slightest hint of dismay.

"Jeff," an older man walked up and said, "I'm going to lunch, want to come along? It's your mother's treat. She and Joanie are in town shopping for the wedding."

Jeff turned and for a quick moment looked at his father, still watching the Orman Building entrance from the corner of his eye. "No, Dad, I've had lunch. I'll just hang around here I guess. Tell Mother and Joanie I'll see them Sunday." He turned back to face the building fully.

"What's this thing with hot dogs, son?" the elder Bannerman asked with passing interest. "This is the second week of hot dogs and milk for lunch. You on some kind of diet?" The speaker stood much shorter than his son, only five ten, his head covered with thinning white hair, his body thickened considerably around the waistline. His face was weathered and lined and wore a somber expression.

Jeff shook his head. "No, no diet." He removed the bright yellow hardhat and wiped his brow with his sleeve. "I've merely developed a taste for Tony's food. He's a pretty good vendor." Lean and lanky, Jeff's dark golden hair was curled with perspiration at his forehead, ears, and neckline, and sharp gray-blue eyes peered out from under dark, straight brows. His clean-shaven features were chiseled and handsome—he had a square clefted chin and his father's full lips and straight nose. A faint trace of a scar rested almost unnoticeably in the right shadow under his prominent cheekbones.

The father's expression was somewhat puzzled. "Well, I'm going to get on or your mother will have ordered me cottage cheese. If the supply truck from

10

Southwestern arrives while I'm gone, make sure they've got the proper size beams this time."

An absentminded smile spread vaguely on Jeff's lips. "Sure, Dad. Go on, enjoy your lunch." Then he watched in quick glances as his father moved away and got into the company pickup with the raised lettering on the door—Bannerman and Son.

With his father gone, he once again turned his full attention to the building across the street, his expression growing more openly disturbed. Twelve-fifteen. In two weeks she had not varied her lunch hour by more than two minutes. He touched his scarred cheek thoughtfully, wondering about the delay. Today he had decided to approach her, to make conversation, to introduce himself and to learn who she was and what she did in the Orman Building so faithfully five days a week from eight until four. He had never been so intrigued by a woman before, least of all by a complete stranger. But neither had he ever seen a woman so perfectly beautiful. He had to know more about her.

He sat again on the edge of the concrete planter containing a small palm tree, his makeshift dining room for the past two weeks. He slouched a bit, bringing one leg up on the planter and wrapping his arms around it, resting his chin on his knee while his other leg dangled over the side, his foot raking the sidewalk back and forth.

Suddenly the door to the building swung open and he rose to his feet as a squint of concern tightened his eyes. She had come through the door arm in arm with a man. She was looking up into the man's face and both of them were laughing, obviously sharing

11

a mutual joke. Jeff froze, stunned by what he saw, his tanned face creasing with surprise as his mouth opened slightly. For two weeks he had watched her and become thoroughly acquainted with her routine. Every morning she arrived at eight, alone, went into the building, and at twelve or shortly thereafter she would leave for lunch, alone. At one she would return to the building, alone, and not leave again until four. And when she left, she left alone. And now, the very day he had decided to approach her, she exited the building on the arm of a man, quite obviously a man she liked very much.

His gaze of surprise followed the couple until they turned at the corner and disappeared from his line of vision. Then he stood very still, for almost five minutes, staring at the corner of the building where they had turned. The oddest feelings were closing in on him. Questions. Sensations. Almost a fear. What if the man were her husband? What if she were married? God, never in two weeks had he thought of that. She had just looked so single.

He inhaled deeply and exhaled slowly. He had sat on his planter long enough, maybe too long, he reproached himself. He wanted to know who she was and what she did in the Orman Building. He even wanted to know who the man was, and what he was to her.

Looking quickly both ways, he jaywalked across the street and hurriedly went into the entrance of the six-story office building in downtown Pensacola, Florida. He found himself at the glassed-in wall register, studying the list of occupants, all professionals, mostly doctors of one kind or another. The building was convenient to the hospital a block away, so he wasn't surprised at the listings.

His eyes touched every name, fleeing over the males. Of the thirty names, four were females. He stared at the list. Maybe he wouldn't find the right one, but he could make only three mistakes before he did. He spread out his long legs and folded his hands neatly behind him, studying the register. She had to be a doctor of some kind; she had come out twice wearing a short white lab coat over her street clothes. Both times, outside the building, she had stopped and slid the jacket off and folded it across her arm as though she had worn it unthinkingly, maybe out of habit.

His eyes rested on the first name and he shook his head, thinking, no, she wasn't Hazel Baker, ob-gyn specialist. She didn't look like a Hazel Baker. His glare moved to the second line. Lisa Malvaney, pediatrician. His eyes again narrowed. Possibly, he thought, she could possibly be a Lisa. But could she be a pediatrician? He visualized the image he had found so enjoyable to watch daily. Pretty, soft features, shiny black hair neatly and skillfully styled at the base of her neck in a knot. No, he thought, not a pediatrician. She was too serene, too delicate in appearance. A pediatrician would have to look more harried.

On he went to the third name. Kasha Lockridge, psychiatry, marriage counseling. Kasha. His lips silently mouthed the single word. Then again. Kasha. He had no other thought at the moment as his eyes read the letters of the fourth and final name. Barbara Kilgore, hematologist. He touched the side of his nose thoughtfully, then pulled at one side of his face. Barbara. But even as he thought about the sound, his eyes went back to the third name. Kasha Lockridge. A psychiatrist. A marriage counselor. Now his entire face wrinkled and he almost groaned aloud.

Several people came and went while he stood facing the names of the building's occupants. Suddenly he wheeled on his heel just as the elevator reached the lobby and a woman carrying a small child in her arms walked out, and behind her a nurse in white uniform. Watching to see if they were together, Jeff decided they weren't and stepped over quickly toward the nurse. "Excuse me, miss," he said, his eyes stopping her with their forcefulness. "Could you help me a moment?"

The shapely nurse paused and looked up at him inquiringly. "What is it?" she asked pleasantly.

Clearing his throat somewhat nervously, he made his shot in the dark. "I—uh—I was wondering about Dr. Lockridge. Could you tell me if she's a—you know—a good psychiatrist?"

The nurse hesitated, scrutinizing him with a tinge more candor. "I don't believe Dr. Lockridge deals as much with psychiatric problems in general as she does with marriage counseling. Her partner, Dr. Wells, is the active psychiatrist in the partnership." Again she hesitated. "Perhaps he's the one you would want to see. I'm almost certain she's mainly involved with marriage counseling," she concluded, moving a bit impatiently in the direction of the door.

"Could you tell me if Dr. Lockridge is the short woman with blond hair?" he called after her.

The nurse reached for the door, then turned back

quickly to look at him, her expression one of mass confusion. "No, Dr. Lockridge is dark-haired. You must be thinking of Dr. Baker, but she's ob-gyn." She started to add something more but decided against continuing the strange conversation. Instead, she gave this inquisitive man a fleeting onceover and hurried on out the door, imparting a last severe glance at him from the outside.

He smiled to himself. He was right. She wasn't a Hazel Baker, she was a Kasha Lockridge. He pursed his lips in a silent whistle and stared bright-eyed at the register. Just the name Kasha Lockridge excited and delighted him.

He stood there a long while, pleased with his detective work. He was smiling gaily, silently whistling "The Most Beautiful Girl in the World" when the glass doors swung open and the lady of his thoughts entered, followed closely by the man who had escorted her out of the building a half-hour earlier. The pucker froze on his lips and he stepped closer to the register, watching her every movement from the corner of his eyes. She was elegantly beautiful and carried herself with a smooth grace that revealed itself in her whole figure.

When she passed close to where he stood he couldn't help looking around at her, and as he looked she, too, turned her head and met his eyes with a fleeting smile on her face before turning back to speak to the man accompanying her. Jeff had seen something so caressingly soft in her features, such a pleasant expression in her shining brown eyes when they looked at him from thick black lashes, that in that brief second of passing he knew beyond all

15

doubts he had to meet her. She fascinated him to such an extent he found himself at a complete loss to understand his own emotions—emotions that under any other circumstances would have alarmed and disturbed him.

He glared blankly out the front doors of the building, concentrating intensely, when something across the street caught his eyes. The supply truck from Southwestern had pulled into the work yard and two men were maneuvering a crane into an unloading position. He jumped forward and in a nimble run dashed back across the street, weaving in and out of the heavy noon traffic.

Kasha Lockridge entered her modern office with a quick glance at her watch. Twelve forty-five. Placing her leather clutch bag in a bottom drawer of her low decorative black desk, she gave a hardly perceptible sigh, and after sliding the drawer shut, touched the center of her forehead with three fingers, rubbing softly. She started to seat herself in the white leather chair to await her next appointment, the Shaws, but unconsciously changed her mind, and picking up a brass paperweight in the shape of a frog, she walked to the window, juggling the frog in one hand. She stared out at the construction site across the street, her gaze settling on the young man pointing at a crane operator. She studied him with a blank expression on her face. She wondered what his problem was. For two weeks she had caught glimpses of him, morning, noon, and afternoon, always alone, always staring at the Orman Building. And then today he had been downstairs in the lobby glaring at the register. She wondered if he had a mental problem of some kind. He certainly behaved as though he might.

She touched her lips thoughtfully, her full attention on him, which was suddenly disrupted by the intercom on her desk announcing, "Dr. Lockridge, Mr. and Mrs. Shaw are here."

Turning her gaze from the window, she moved slowly back to her desk and placed the brass frog on a stack of memos. Walking over to the small closet at the back of the office, she removed a freshly laundered white jacket, slipping it on over her navy and white cotton dress. She didn't usually wear it, but this was going to be a difficult session, and she wanted to look particularly authoritative. Then she seated herself behind the curved desk, waited a moment, then answered in a low voice, "Send them in, please, Chandra."

As she awaited the battling Shaws, her eyes swept around the room's modern Oriental decor; the two low sofas separated by a brass and bamboo table with an elegant Chinese lamp, the delicate Oriental paintings on the wall above the sofas blending in harmony with the white designer furniture and the soft rust-colored carpet.

The door clicked and she looked up to see two of her unhappiest patients. She shivered inwardly, thinking the unthinkable. *I don't know if I can help these two save their marriage.* The counseling sessions had not yet resulted in true open communication between the two parties. And at this point she had doubts that it ever would. In past sessions they had talked around the problems with what little conversation they could muster.

17

"Please sit down." She smiled warmly at the couple and watched thoughtfully as each one selected a sofa, deliberately avoiding being close to the other. She always watched for this in her patients. It was the first sign that therapy wasn't working. She mentally reviewed the alternatives she had considered since the last session with the Shaws, then discarded the batch. A month had already proven that time wasn't the miracle cure in this case. If anything, time had served to widen the gap. She paused thoughtfully before directing her question to Alice Shaw. "How are your children, Alice?"

The thirty-five-year-old curly-haired woman gave her a long, troubled gaze before answering. "They are both fine now. Sammy is eating again and Ginger is beginning to talk to her daddy sometimes. They are both at such emotional ages, twelve and thirteen. I think it's been as hard on them as it has been on Brad and myself. There's such tension when we're all together, like four sticks of dynamite that might explode at any given moment."

"Brad?" Kasha turned her attention to the husband, who was glaring at the carpet. Brad Shaw was a clean-cut, trim man in his middle thirties, an insurance adjuster for a leading company.

He lifted his face abruptly, but would not meet Kasha's eyes. Instead, he glared past her with a grimace on his face. "I don't think it's working and I don't think it ever will. Nobody can forget. The kids both look at me like I'm some kind of creep. I feel like we've lost all hope of communicating and nothing's going to get it back."

Bewilderment rose in Alice Shaw's voice as she

18

interrupted before he could say more. "You're not trying, Brad!" she exclaimed, her voice heightening. "At least the children and I are trying! That's more than you can say! You're like a zombie in the house. You don't talk or laugh or joke. You just mope around like you're all alone in the world."

Lowering his head, he lapsed back into silence, his eyes again on the carpet.

An hour later, after the Shaws had left the office, Kasha again thought of many things she could have said to the floundering couple, but truthfully doubted that any one word would have helped. She hit her lower teeth with the back of her thumbnail in quick little taps, knowing that the opportunity to help this marriage was entering the "no-help" zone.

She did not even look up when Chandra walked in to bring the next file and announce that the second afternoon appointment was already in the waiting room.

Thankfully, the remainder of the scheduled appointments was more rewarding. At a few minutes before four Kasha found herself preparing to leave the day's work behind. She opened the desk drawer and removed her purse, setting it on top of the desk. She started to rise from her chair when the intercom buzzed again. "Yes, what is it?" she inquired of her receptionist.

"Dr. Lockridge, there's a man out here who wants to see you." Chandra hesitated. "He says it's urgent."

"Do we have a file on him?" came the automatic reply.

"No, this is his first visit. His name is Mr. Bannerman. Mr. Jeffrey Bannerman."

Kasha heard a male voice in the background. "Tell her it's a matter of life or death."

"All right, Chandra, I'll see him. Please prepare me a file. And you may leave at your regular time." She clicked off the intercom and sat back in her cushioned chair with a long sigh. It was always against her better judgment to refuse to see anyone who seemed so in need.

With a somber expression she sat back and waited. And after what seemed close to an eternity, the door opened and Chandra walked in holding a manila folder in her hand. Placing it on the corner of the desk, she whispered, "If this is a true emergency, I'll eat this file first thing in the morning." She flipped around and coolly eyed the young man entering the office, then sped past him and closed the door with a loud click.

Kasha eyed the tall handsome man dressed neatly in an olive green lightweight suit, white shirt, and small-patterned tie. He had dark golden hair and deep, flashing gray-blue eyes that smiled brightly at her. Strange as it seemed, for some unknown reason he looked vaguely familiar to her. With rapid movements she placed his file before her and opened it, then was at a complete loss at what she discovered. Apparently the man wasn't even married. She stared at the data sheet a moment, then looked quizzically at him. "Mr. Bannerman, I'm afraid you might have come to the wrong office," she declared in a soft voice, a quick gaze resting on him before casting her

20

eyes again to the information sheet. "It states here that you aren't married."

He flashed sparkling white teeth at her lowered head. Then when she raised her eyes his smile vanished and he took on a half-desperate expression. "No, I'm not," he admitted, approaching her desk. "I came to see you."

She clasped her hands together and stared at him with a faint smile. "Well, I'm a counselor for married couples. I think maybe Dr. Wells is the one you should see."

"No." He spoke firmly with a quick shake of his head. "I came to see you. Dr. Kasha Lockridge, marriage counselor," he answered with a look of concern furrowing his brow. "I believe you're the only person in the world who can help me. There are very special reasons why I felt it necessary to seek your thoughts on some matters," he continued with his explanation. "It'll save us problems after we're married."

She raised her chin and her dark, heavily fringed eyes glared in puzzlement. "Are you saying that you're having problems before your marriage?"

For a long moment his eyes held hers, then looked around quickly at the office walls. "Well—uh—my situation is somewhat difficult to explain," he began in a low voice. "And I get terrible vibrations in a doctor's office." He looked again at the classic beauty of her face, then had to fight to keep her from seeing the desire that surged upward from the pit of his stomach. "Do you think you could accompany me down the block to Selana's or across to Gilio's? It

21

would be so much easier to talk with you across a table."

She caught her breath. "What?" The single word relayed her surprise.

"Go out with me," he said with a slight smile, "away from this office."

His request both alarmed and intrigued her. For all she knew he could be a modern-day Jack the Ripper in an olive suit, but for some reason she didn't feel wary of him. Still, she answered with, "I'm afraid that's out of the question." She looked again to the folder and added, "Mr. Bannerman." She wanted to know about his problem, but she wouldn't leave her office with him.

At that moment her phone rang. "Excuse me, please," she said, lifting the receiver and saying, "Dr. Lockridge."

Jeff's gaze roamed over her as she talked. She was so exquisitely beautiful, and he had already screwed up royally. With a feeling of dismay he walked over to the nearest sofa and lowered himself onto it, listening to her end of the conversation and wondering why she wore a white lab coat. He knew most professionals in the counseling end of medical practice didn't, and he wondered why she did. But his thoughts of the short white coat slipped away when he heard her say: "Yes, Roman, I will. No, I'll just meet you at the club. All right, dear, see you at eight." She carefully replaced the receiver and glanced around for her patient, finding him seated on the sofa with a dejected expression.

Jeff's heart sank even lower. Roman Wells, her

partner. He remembered reading the name on the register.

"All right, Jeff." She eyed him with a fleeting smile. "Are you ready to talk about your problem?"

He seemed to search for a moment before he said, "Why do you wear that coat?"

She gazed at him in silence.

"I mean," he went on in a level voice, "most people in your field don't anymore, do they?"

"Why do you ask?" Her large eyes widened. "Does the coat bother you?" *If so,* she thought, *too bad.* She wasn't going to take it off for him.

Jeff heaved a sigh, then said, "Oh, no, it doesn't. But I thought the white coat created barriers between doctor and patient." He shrugged. "I must have read it somewhere."

Kasha chose her words carefully, her voice noticeably firm. "It is my belief and has always been, Jeff, that there is a difference between the therapist and the client." She picked up her pen and held it idly. "If this coat makes that difference seem more acute, I assure you it's only so in the beginning sessions." She pursed her lips together for a brief moment before saying, "If it bothers you—"

"No, it doesn't bother me," he interrupted quickly. "Nothing about you bothers me." His eyes caught hers and held. "You aren't married, are you?" he asked softly, knowing fate could not be that unkind to him.

Dropping her pen onto the desk, she was about to clasp her long, tapered fingers together, but halted her hand in midair. "No," she replied, then clasped

23

her hands together, returning a question. "Why do you ask?"

Instantly he abandoned his plan of deceit. "Because I'm in love with you," he said firmly. "And that's the only problem I have."

Her mouth opened, then clamped shut. She thought she had encountered everything, but this was a new one on her. A total stranger had walked into her office, questioned her about her lab coat, and then openly declared his love for her. Obviously the lab coat had failed to create the proper barrier. This was a first. She felt herself flush, and though she tried to smile coolly, she couldn't conceal her shock.

He glared at her with open earnestness. "I've watched you come and go every day. At first I thought, My what a pretty woman. And then I made a point to watch you. I love everything about you—the way you look, the way you walk." His eyes sought her face quickly and he continued. "Sitting here now, I know that you're everything I think you are. And I've got to know you better." He shrugged and smiled lovingly at her. "It's fate."

She stared at him breathlessly with open-mouthed disbelief. Now she knew him. He was the man she had seen downstairs earlier, the man who had watched the building day after day. It was startling to know he had been watching her. She had wondered what his problem was—and now that she knew, she wasn't sure how to handle him. Her eyes evaded his. "I'm afraid I'm at a loss for words, Jeff. If—if this is some kind of joke, I assure you I don't find it to be at all funny."

He rose silently to his feet. His hand wandered up

24

the front of his suit and he clutched his lapel. "It's no joke. Here—I'll show you—it's no joke."

"Oh, no!" she exclaimed softly, but firmly, raising one hand, signaling him to stop. "Stay where you are." As she watched him move toward her desk, she drew away in her chair, declaring in a firmer tone, "Don't come near me." She waved the hand as if to ward him off. "Please, leave!"

Without a word he walked behind the desk and pulled her up to him as she frantically tried to disengage herself from his strong hold.

"Brute strength doesn't impress me!" she choked out as he bent his head to her face. And then she didn't try to fight him. She stood passively in his arms, eyeing him. The cold glare had always worked previously and she was bestowing two iced-over irises at him. Then she felt the first touch of his lips, quick as lightning, brushing hers. Now she was genuinely alarmed.

"I have dreamed about you," he whispered, and his lips brushed hers again and his arms around her changed from a gentle touch to a clasp of iron. "I've dreamed about you. Can you believe that? Really, we aren't strangers."

Not daring to inquire into the nature of his dreams, she tried again unsuccessfully to free herself of his arms, then once more resolved to be passive, keeping darkening cool eyes fixed on him, her body drawing away from his as much as possible. "Let me go," she said tensely, her eyes narrowing.

"If you'll kiss me one time, I'll let you go," he whispered close to her face. "I promise."

He smiled and she was gripped by the thought that

25

only piano keys should be so white and perfect. Then she averted her head downward with a quick angry nod. "I will not compromise with you, Mr. Bannerman. And you will let me go immediately," she replied stonily, now more acutely conscious of his nearness, shocked because for a moment she had considered complying with his ultimatum. Indignantly she swept her face aside, as if it were painful to look at him.

When she did, his strong arms tightened and he leaned forward, kissing her softly, this time on the neck, a slow, burning touch that gave her such a start her head swung back around so that she looked him straight in the eye. "If you do that again, I will scream," she said flatly, professionally.

He spoke, his voice extraordinarily deep and soft, hardly audible. "I love you," he insisted. "There's no use to waste a lot of time before I tell you—because I do, and I have, probably from that first moment I saw you."

Her voice suddenly rose. "Don't say that again. In the first place, it isn't true, and in the second place, there's no way it could be. You don't even know me." She had never been in such a predicament. What in the world was she going to do? She had to first get him out of her office, and when that was done she would clearly chart a plan of action. She swallowed hard, regaining control of the volume in which she spoke. "I will admit that you have a problem." Again she swallowed. "And I will try and see that you receive help on a professional basis. But only if you release me this instant," she added emphatically, suddenly aware that her partner, Roman Wells, was about to get himself a new case. One, Mr. Jeffrey Bannerman.

He held fast to her a moment longer, then slowly his grip loosened and a glint appeared in the gray-blue irises. "You mean you'll see me as a patient?" His voice was soft, almost cajoling.

"I said that I would be responsible for you receiving help," she retorted, now feeling in control of the situation, but still a bit stunned by her agreement to see him again, even though it was only to make him leave her office. She would make him an "emergency" appointment with Roman first thing in the morning. Roman was much better qualified to deal with this type of problem.

He watched her expression closely. "Tomorrow?" he asked. "Same time?"

"We'll have to see," she answered cautiously, avoiding his eyes.

"I have to know," he said with suddenness.

"All right," she lied convincingly, knowing full well that she was lying. But he gave her no alternative. She had to convince him of her truthfulness in order to get him out of her office. "I'll see you tomorrow, but never again after hours. Check with my receptionist in the morning and she'll fit you into the schedule. And, Mr. Bannerman," she hesitated, feeling her neck muscles tighten, "there are ground rules that must be followed." She now backed a step from him, continuing with, "First, you must stop watching me. Second, you must consider me only as your therapist. Thirdly, there will be no more physical contact. Agreed?" So, she was lying, but it didn't matter. After all, she was doing only what was good for him.

"Agreed," he returned immediately with an oddly respectful smile. "I'll be your best patient."

She watched him as objectively as possible as he moved to the door. Before he went out he gave her one last charming smile, his bright eyes shining. "See you tomorrow."

She stood, watching the door close behind him, making no comment. After he was gone she lowered herself back into her chair and whispered, "No, you won't. You have just concluded your only session with me." She pursed her lips again, then relaxed them into a smile with the thought, *Tomorrow will be a new day for you—and Roman Wells.*

## CHAPTER TWO

Her deep brown eyes followed the whitecaps sweeping inland to wet the snow-white sand in a foaming swirl before flowing out again to the dark Gulf waters. Preoccupied with her thoughts, she sat in silence, holding a lobster cracker in her right hand, the untouched lobster growing cool on her plate. She and her date, Roman Wells, had arrived at the beach club an hour earlier for dinner, and even a short stroll out on the pier had not increased her hunger.

Roman looked over at her thoughtfully. He was a tall, thin man with sharp features accentuated by a straight, narrow moustache over thin lips. His small piercing black eyes followed hers out to sea before coming back to gaze at her plate. "That kook really upset you, didn't he?" he asked finally, placing his fork on his plate and holding his fingers together in a steeple.

She frowned momentarily, then replied indifferently, "Oh, I don't know if upset is the proper word. I'm merely surprised at how unprepared I am to cope adequately with such situations." She looked intently over at him, her eyes widening. "I tell you, Roman, for a moment I was at a total loss to do anything." She sat up on her chair and leaned forward over the table slightly, shaking her head. "For a moment I found myself completely off balance. He's such a handsome man—blond, beautiful eyes, and the whitest teeth I've ever seen."

Roman's brows rose. "You didn't enjoy his kiss, did you, Kasha?" he asked with a noticeable tinge of alarm.

"Of course not," she replied, obviously shocked by the question. "How could you even ask?"

He gave a short laugh. "You have talked of little else since I arrived to pick you up."

"Well," she said with a hint of annoyance, "I'm sorry. I didn't realize you wouldn't be interested."

Another short laugh. "Oh, I'm interested, but I think you're making too much of it. What I see is a man employed in construction, which is an earthy type of occupation, who has seen a perfectly gorgeous woman, a type of woman probably unfamiliar to his life-style, but nevertheless a woman he has begun to worship from afar. I feel comfortable with predicting that he possesses schizophrenic tendencies, and in order to extricate himself from the unpleasant reality of his life, he has created a mental illusion of a perfect love. And in that illusion you are the perfect love. Undoubtedly the man needs counseling." He went on smoothly. "But you've done right in referring him to me, because it's obvious that you would be the one person least likely to help him."

She sighed. "You're right, of course. But, Roman, I don't feel that he's schizophrenic."

Roman's eyes enlarged slightly. "Oh, really. And what was your diagnosis?" he almost snapped at her.

"Oh," Kasha said breezily, "I feel it's something much more simple. Perhaps he's one of that small percentage of our population prone to falling in love at first sight. He truly didn't appear to be neurotic or psychotic."

Roman held up one hand. "I've read those studies on the love-at-first-sight syndrome and if he's one of those, he would probably be better off to be schizophrenic. At least we can now treat psychoses." His thin dark brows rose. "I don't believe a cure for love at first sight has been perfected. Those people are not capable of forming lasting relationships. They simply fall in love with every Tom, Dick, and Harry, or in your client's particular case, every Jane, Mae, and Sally they meet." He sighed heavily. "It's unfortunate, but this small group believes that it is sex that endures, not trust or the other needed emotions that truly make romantic love last." He shook his head and again sighed. "If this is the case with your young man, I would say that his prognosis is indeed bleak. He probably began falling in love at first sight at a very young age, and now he goes where his body chemistry leads him." Roman's facial features lengthened. "Sad, isn't it?"

Kasha hadn't thought so up until now, but it was truly sad. She had never wished a psychotic condition on a patient before, but the thought of that handsome man crawling in and out of beds in his unrequited search for love made her feel that one malady was as devastating as the other.

Her eyes again went back to the shoreline and she

suddenly shivered. It had been an exasperating day, a bewildering day, and she felt a bit weighted down by it all.

Roman asked quietly, "Would you like me to get your wrap, or perhaps move to a table inside? I see you're shivering."

She smiled. "My wrap, if you don't mind. I don't want to move inside."

Again placing his fork on his plate, he rose from his chair.

Her eyes trailed after him until his tall frame disappeared inside. She raised her hands and rested her chin on folded fingers, her eyes sweeping up to the bright moon overhead, black-fringed eyes sparkling as she sighed softly.

Slowly her eyes came back from the sky and automatically scanned the table beyond Roman's empty chair. For an instant there was acute surprise on her face. Her lips parted as her eyes widened. She swallowed. Directly across from her sat Jeffrey Bannerman, neatly attired in black dinner jacket, white shirt, black tie, seated opposite a strikingly attractive young woman with hair almost the color of his. For a moment she thought, *He followed me. He followed me here.* Then her bewildered mind knew that didn't make any sense. If he were following her, why would he drag another woman along, particularly a young woman whose company he seemed to be enjoying immensely. She could not catch their words, but they were laughing, talking, obviously having a delightful time. She sat staring at him, an incredibly puzzled expression on her face. Suddenly he looked around and for a moment white teeth gleamed at her in the wavering candlelight of his table. Her eyes dropped immediately to the decorative candle glass on her table, then a moment later she shifted in her chair, turning to face the Gulf.

Roman returned and placed the wrap across her shoulders, peering down at her. "Is that better?" he asked quietly, resting one hand on her shoulder.

She reached up and covered his hand with hers, saying almost in a whisper, "Much. Thanks." She squeezed his fingers, then her hand slid back to join the other in her lap.

When Roman reseated himself, she smiled uneasily at him, her eyes flickering momentarily above his shoulder at the tanned face no longer smiling at her. With a satisfied sigh, she mentioned to Roman, "Their band is very good."

His dark eyes brightened at her. "Yes. They're new. They're enlisted men from Eglin Air Force Base. This is their first night here."

The rich sound of "I Left My Heart in San Francisco" sifted out from the indoor dining room. She leaned forward and said, "That's one of my favorites, why don't we da—"

The maître d's quick approach at the table stopped her in mid-word. "Dr. Wells," he said softly. "You have a call from the hospital. Would you like the phone out here?"

Roman rose swiftly. "No, I'll take it inside. Excuse me, Kasha."

Still open-mouthed, she watched him disappear again through the open terrace doors. Grimacing, she straightened the skirt of her long dinner gown,

33

taking caution not to glance at the table opposite or its occupants.

The next moment she felt fingers on her elbow. Her head jerked up sharply to the handsome devil-may-care face glancing down at her. "They're playing our song," he said casually as his fingers pressed into the flesh of her arm.

She stared impersonally and replied dryly, "I don't believe *we* have a song, Mr. Bannerman."

He smiled. "Every couple needs a song. We'll make this one ours."

"No," she said emphatically. "Doctors and patients rarely select songs, or consider themselves couples. Now, please go back to your table."

"Would you mind not embarrassing me in the presence of my date," he said with a sigh. "You see, she thinks I'm wonderful."

She shifted away from his touch, freeing her arm. He was in worse shape than she thought. He might even fit into that exclusive category of victims of love who fell for more than one person at a time. Only hours ago he had vowed his love for her, Kasha Lockridge, and now he was in the club with another woman who thought he was "wonderful." And that woman was most likely the one with whom he needed to dance. "I'm sorry," Kasha began, "but I—"

"I won't take no," he interrupted with a sure smile and whispered softly, "Dance with me, Doctor. I won't step on your toes."

She eyed him caustically, knowing that a person with his condition rarely stepped on toes, rather they stamped on hearts. "I'm sorry," she said again, but before she could continue found herself almost pulled from the chair.

She glanced a bit helplessly at the young woman at the table who sat watching with a warm pleasant expression on her face. The woman didn't appear to mind that her date was literally dragging another woman from her table, so Kasha supposed rather than create a scene she would comply with his wishes.

With some hesitation she allowed him to escort her toward the dance floor. His hand went down and captured hers in a strong clasp, and when he squeezed gently she felt a strange, most unwelcome current travel up her arm.

At the edge of the dance floor, he stopped and turned her to him, slipping one arm under her wrap, slowly drawing her closer. Her right hand still rested in his. Eyes met and he smiled somewhat mischievously. Her expression remained grim.

"You don't mind if I tell you how great you look, do you?" he said softly.

"I most certainly do mind," she returned haughtily.

"Okay," he said with a quick laugh. "I won't tell you. And I also won't tell you that I think you're the most beautiful woman alive." His eyes sparkled in the moonlight as he smiled, his bronze skin crinkling at the corners of his eyes. "And lastly, I won't even tell you how wonderful it is to hold you this way."

The soft melody of the music settled around their heads and bodies swayed gracefully to the slow rhythm. She could feel his lean body drawing closer with the magnetic effect of his arm tightening on her waist. "Not so close," she whispered harshly, realizing her heart was beginning to unleash a new rhythm of its own. Thoroughly alarmed at her response to the lean gentle touch of his body against hers, she flattened one hand on his chest, pushing back from his embrace. Somewhat breathlessly she glared at him and frowned. "I said, not so close," came the hot whisper.

"Sorry," he replied, grinning, his gaze locking on hers. "I suppose I got carried away. It won't happen again."

"It certainly will not. This dance has ended. Permanently."

Magically, as her words stopped, so did the music. He stood holding her, making no move to drop his arm from her waist, or escort her back to her table.

"Could we talk a minute?" he inquired.

"Absolutely not. I would like to return to my table. And you should devote your attention to your young lady." Clasping his arms firmly, she removed herself from his embrace and swept quickly back to her table where she sat down, then turned, glaring anxiously out over the water, and tapped the polished stone floor impatiently with her heel. She refused herself so much as a glance at the table across from her.

She felt a growing irritation with Roman. He had been inside long enough to speak personally with each nurse on staff at Seaview. As much as she hated to think it, she wondered if her colleague didn't enjoy being singled out in crowds perhaps a bit too much. She had yet to go anywhere with him when he had not received an "emergency" telephone call. She no-

36

ticed it happened every time, at the theater, at restaurants, in the club. *Dr. Roman Wells, please report here and there and everywhere.* It was one of the things that kept her from getting too involved with him.

She began immediately tapping her lower teeth with the back of her thumbnail, a nervous quirk she had fought since high school. Realizing what she was doing, she halted her thumb at her lip, then allowed her hand to slowly slide down to her lap.

She could feel his eyes burning into the side of her face. The cool Gulf breeze sweeping her face neutralized the flush rising slowly to her cheeks. Jeffrey Bannerman, she thought, was a nice-looking man, obviously too nice-looking for his own mental health. She found herself pondering the deep-seated basis of his problem. What had gone awry in his youth, his childhood? Normal, healthy men just didn't walk up to total strangers and openly proclaim love, at least not any of the normal, healthy men she knew. Still, she reluctantly had to admit there was something a bit intriguing about the overall man. And certainly his tough, lanky body emitted anything but insanity. Annoyed with herself, she sighed heavily.

Finally Roman returned, dramatically beginning his apology several steps from the table. "Forgive me, Kasha. I had no idea I would be tied up so long."

Irked, she glanced up, her voice flat. "A patient?"

He lowered himself into his chair and cleared his throat. "Yes. You remember me telling you about Mrs. Brent?"

Kasha glanced at him wordlessly.

37

He went on. "Well, tonight she decided to be difficult. She refused her nine o'clock medication."

Tonelessly she questioned him. "You mean they called you because a patient would not take her medicine? Your dinner was interrupted for that?"

He looked anxiously over at her. "Naturally. I want to be notified whenever a patient begins to deviate from the norm."

Perfectly knowledgeable of the fact the patient in question had not had a normal day in her life, Kasha lapsed into a disgruntled silence. She could not recall ever feeling so totally exasperated.


Jeffrey Bannerman watched her walk from the terrace, Roman Wells's hand pressing her back. She had glanced quickly at him one time during the departure and he had watched her leave solemn-faced.

He finally turned his attention back to the young woman opposite him at the table. "What do you think?"

The woman shook her blond head. "It's hard to say, Jeff. She's pretty, but she didn't appear to be overly fond of you."

He smiled with confidence. "Joanie, she just met me today. I'll grant you she's a bit skeptical, but time will cure her skepticism."

Joanie looked intently at him, then asked bluntly, "What are you up to, Jeff? And I mean really. I want to know."

He laughed, raising his brows. "Now, is that any question to ask of your older brother? I'm in love with the woman. She thinks I'm a bit off center right now, but in a few days she'll realize that it's for real."

38

She continued to eye him suspiciously. "Why didn't you go about this in a normal manner? Introductions, dates, the getting-to-know-each-other routine that's worked for millions of people over the years? It worked for me and Donald. It worked for Mom and Dad. Wally and Debbie. I think you've gone about it the wrong way. If I were in her place, I would always look at you through a jaundiced eye, if you know what I mean." She glanced at her watch. "I need to go. Don's supposed to call when he gets back at midnight."

He smiled. "Okay. I certainly wouldn't want you to miss a call from your beloved. Thanks for coming with me tonight. It would have been obvious that I followed her if I had been alone." He winked. "I owe you one."

She shook her head, saying, "Don't mention it." Her eyes widened. "And I mean that literally. Don't mention it to Mom or Dad, or anyone, or I might be going to counseling with you."

He laughed, placing his arm around her and squeezing her to his side. "I hope Don realizes what he's getting here. I mean you're blue ribbon."

Both laughing softly, they entered the main dining room where to his surprise he saw Kasha standing at the front desk, and a foot or so from her, her escort holding a phone to his ear.

Seeing him, Kasha's mouth fell apart slightly. Slowly his arm slid from around Joanie and he straightened as he guided her by the pair at the desk, his eyes not moving from the lovely oval face with the wide dark eyes and full sensual lips that were

39

drawn in a definite line. She was tall, slim, curved, everything. She was something.

He hesitated after passing her, left Joanie, walked back to her, and asked quickly, "Having any trouble here?"

She cut her eyes coolly at him. "No. Thank you."

At that point Roman covered the end of the receiver with his palm and interrupted his phone conversation to say, "She's with me."

Jeff looked strangely at him. "Then you better see to her, buddy boy, because I'm about to steal her right from under your nose."

Jolted, Roman craned his neck, muttered a few words into the receiver, and slammed it down. Turning abruptly to Jeff, he said, "I beg your pardon!"

Jeff shrugged. "Don't beg my pardon, it's this beautiful woman with you whose pardon you should beg."

"Sir," Roman threw out hostilely, "I would appreciate you minding your own business!"

Openly surprised at Roman's loss of control, Kasha's mouth parted as she shot a warning glance at Jeff.

Jeff held her eyes a moment before moving away into the crowded entrance hall to find Joanie.

Kasha pulled her wrap tighter across her breast and wordlessly she and Roman walked from the restaurant.

"I assume that man was someone you once knew?" Roman mumbled, unlocking the car door on her side.

"Hmmm, slightly," she replied innocently.

"A lifeguard?" Roman pursued sarcastically, walking around the front of the car to his side.

He got in before she answered. "No. What makes you ask?" she inquired with sudden interest.

Placing the key in the ignition, he looked over at her. "He looked like a beach bum, an over-aged lifeguard."

She sat strangely silent. She was surprised that Roman's remark had set off a new spark of anger in her. Most likely now she would not refer Jeff Bannerman to him for therapy. If she couldn't adequately plan a course of treatment for him, she would have to refer him to the clinic, completely bypassing Roman Wells. Besides, now that she hadn't admitted who he was, she couldn't refer him to Roman anyway. He would question her evasiveness concerning his identity. And she certainly wasn't about to undergo a session with Roman.

All her plans had been messed up and now she had no idea what to do about Jeffrey Bannerman. She would just squeal, if it weren't so unprofessional.

# CHAPTER THREE

The next morning Kasha walked from her beach-front condominium, her hands thrust into the large pockets of her lightweight beige range jacket. A stiff Gulf breeze slapped the back of her head as she glanced up at the cloudy sky, seeking a first glint of sunlight, but finding none.

Sliding into her car in the first of the row of garages behind the building, she turned the ignition, leaned forward, and popped a tape into the player, then slowly backed down the long drive. She wasn't exactly happy this morning, but she couldn't decipher why not.

Glancing again at the sky once she had started down the two-lane highway leading to Pensacola Beach, she told herself it was the weather. Cloudy dark skies always dampened her moods. She was basically a sunshine person. Stiffening behind the wheel, she chided herself harshly for evading the real issue promoting her foul mood of the morning. It was that fool—Jeffrey Bannerman.

She breathed in deeply. Her mind was made up. She wasn't going to treat him or refer him to Roman Wells. In his arms dancing, she had diagnosed him as suffering from the "caveman" syndrome. Today she would send him and his prehistoric ideas of love back across the street so fast it would make his head spin, before he took it upon himself to drag her from the building by the hair of her head. "Fool," she grunted aloud.

Reaching into her pocket, she removed a breakfast bar and slowly unwrapped it. Taking a bite, it crumbled; nuts, raisins, and bits of chocolate dropped onto her light ivory skirt. "Oh, damn." Slowing the car, she took one hand and swept the particles from her skirt. Angrily she deposited the remainder of the bar in the litter container and looked despairingly down at the two dark stains across her lap. She automatically considered immediate alternatives—drive back and change clothes or wear the full-length lab coat hanging in her closet, the coat she despised because it was long and tacky. She had been meaning to hem it for months, maybe today between appointments she would manage to do just that.

She pulled into the building parking lot without so much as a glimpse at the construction site across the street. The thought of seeing him standing there gawking at her made her positively ill. He had kept her from a good night's sleep; wild crazy thoughts leaped across her mind at all hours.

Keeping her head turned in the direction of her building, she hurried in and stepped into the elevator. On the way up to her suite she tried to rework the expression on her face for Chandra's benefit. The receptionist had never seen her ruffled, but always the cool, assured professional.

"Morning, Chandra," she said lightly, breezing

into the office. Suddenly a movement on the sofa caught her eye and she looked, then gasped. Jeffrey Bannerman sat relaxed in work khakis, his hands gripping a magazine.

He grinned up over the top of the pages and said, "Hi."

Speechless, she glanced first to him again, then to Chandra, who was peering wide-eyed at her.

She said calmly, "Mr. Bannerman said you said to work him in today, and the only opening we had is now."

Kasha felt her face reddening, but said nothing.

Chandra went on. "The Normans canceled so you won't have anyone until the Clarks at nine thirty."

Feeling a sudden bewilderment, she gave her head a little shake. "I see," she returned fretfully. She had rather Chandra had not revealed that she was free for an hour and a half. Edging toward the door, she said back over her shoulder, "I'll be with you in a moment, Mr. Bannerman."

Shutting her office door behind her, she leaned against it, knowing her face was hot as flames. The very idea of him! He had ruined her night and now was about to do the same thing to her day. Flinging off the jacket, she moved to the closet and pulled on the long lab coat, muttering under her breath, "This is it, buddy boy. Whether you know it or not, your final session is about to commence."

Giving herself a little pep talk, she walked back to the door and opened it. "Mr. Bannerman," she called out coolly.

Swift steps brought him into her office. She closed

the door, her eyes quickly glancing sideways to his eager, confident face.

A sharp tap on the door startled Kasha and when she opened it, Chandra said with a smile, "His file, Dr. Lockridge."

"Thank you, Chandra," she returned, and again closed the door.

He flashed white teeth at her. "I can't imagine a better way to start a day."

Ignoring him, she walked behind the desk.

He remained standing in the middle of the floor, halfway between the desk and the door.

She seated herself and moved her chair forward until the desk touched her middle. Without a hint of a smile she opened his folder.

Switching from one foot to the other, he asked, "Would you like for me to sit on the sofa or in one of these chairs?"

Without lifting her eyes she said vaguely, "Whichever you prefer, or you might just stand, because this won't take long." She inhaled deeply.

Before she could speak he took a step to the desk and inquired softly, "You live out on Santa Rosa Island, don't you?"

Her head jerked and her eyes widened with surprise.

When she didn't reply he went on. "I've been considering buying a house there myself. Do you like it?"

A frown drew her eyebrows almost together and she said shortly, "I don't think that's an idea you should entertain, Mr. Bannerman."

"Jeff," he said quickly, then continued with enthusiasm, "I don't know why I haven't already done it, it's beautiful. We built some of the condos on the bay side last year. I thought about buying a place then."

Inwardly she was conscious of a sudden alarm. Of everyone in the world, she desired him least for a neighbor. She tried to dissuade him by stating, "It isn't perfect there by any means. It's impossible to keep sand out of the house and it's terrifying during storms. I wouldn't advise it at all," she concluded sharply.

He was silent a moment or two, then edged to the chair near her desk and sat down. "I want to be there. I think we would make excellent neighbors."

Now openly disturbed, she exclaimed, "There are few advantages, believe me. For a fact, it's really tiresome after a while. I've been thinking of moving inland myself."

He looked at her with a boyishly simple smile, his hand stretching over the desk to clasp hers firmly. "Why are you fighting this, Kasha?" he asked softly. "I've known for weeks that you're the woman for me. I knew the first time I saw you. I knew yesterday, and last night. I know now."

Strong hands held hers and she felt a warmth run through her veins. She jerked her hand quickly from his clasp. "Jeffrey, aren't you a little old to be dealing in fantasies?" she asked bluntly.

He straightened in the chair and grinned at her. "You're real, aren't you?"

Her voice was dry, decisive. "Yes, I'm real. But that has absolutely nothing to do with the fact that you're deluding yourself, creating a relationship in

46

your mind that will never materialize in reality. I can tell you now in clear terms that I will never become involved with you. I couldn't possibly allow such a thing to occur. Now, I'm being honest with you when I say I can't help you. You definitely need help, but not from me. I'm going to refer you to the clinic at Seaview for further counseling. Undoubtedly something in your past has brought you to this point."

Conscious of the fact he was rising from his chair, she stopped speaking. Not knowing by the sudden change of expression on his face whether he was about to storm out of the office, she watched open-mouthed. It all happened so fast she couldn't be sure what really did happen. She suddenly found herself in his arms, looking at him wildly.

He said slowly, "It isn't anything in my past, it's something in my present—you. You think I'm joking, playing some kind of game. I'm not."

She stood paralyzed while his strong arms slid up the sleeves of her lab coat. "Now, send me anywhere you want; we'll even go visit Freud's tomb if you like, but I want you here from this day forward—in my arms, in my life."

She stirred finally. "This is the second time you've done this, Jeff, and I want it to stop! Now!" An untapped source of power flowed into her and she stiffened. "However, if you expect me to act shocked, I assure you I am about to disappoint you."

She didn't see the frown she expected on his face; instead, he smiled, whispering, "You could never disappoint me, so don't waste your time by trying."

47

She said firmly, "I want you to release me this moment."

He grinned, then whispered, "You know, Kasha, I have the suspicion that somewhere beneath that big coat beats a heart as warm and human as any heart." While he spoke his arms bound her closer to him. "And that's what I want from you. It's all I want—your heart."

Before her parted lips could answer, his mouth covered hers in a kiss that sent her senses reeling. Her first reaction was anger. How dare he kiss her in such a manner! His mouth on hers was no gentle brush of lips. She felt devoured.

Panicked, her lips grew firm, fighting his touch. Her hands pushed hard against his shoulders. Still, he held her pressed close to him, his lips softening, capturing her tight mouth over and over. She tried to utter words to make him stop, but she could not force them past the choking in her throat.

His embrace widened, one arm around her waist, the other at her shoulders, pulling her into the contours of his body until she clearly felt the muscles of his thighs, the expanse of his chest burning into her breasts. And all the while he kissed her, he was doing his damnedest to force her to kiss him. She told herself, she vowed in a silent scream, that she would not. If she never accomplished another feat in her entire life, she would not kiss him.

Fighting to hold her emotions intact, she did not like the sensations coming to life inside her. She felt hot and cold, felt her fingers grow limp at his shoulders, felt her knees weakening.

Then he whispered against her lips, "Kiss me."

The single word "No," formed, and when her lips parted to free it, his tongue moved leisurely, touching her mouth in a slow hot circle. She jerked her head back and he bent forward, his lips traveling along her throat in soft pliant caresses. Again he straightened and captured her mouth with his and she felt the quake start at her knees, a trembling that made her acutely aware that her defenses were leaving her.

She tried to stiffen, but couldn't. *Don't do it,* she told herself. The doctor in her cried out, *You won't be helping him, you'll only make matters worse.* But she was losing it all under the onslaught of his mouth. She knew all the arguments against, and none for. And knowing all that, she kissed him, simply because she no longer had the self-restraint to prevent it.

Slowly her mouth softened, her fingers edged upward, swirling into the silky curves of his hair, then down to the sides of his face. The touch of his hair and the feel of his skin under her fingertips were new sensations for her, awakening a desire she had not experienced before. Her heart had gone awry. She could hear the rapid thudding in her own ears. If she had reached up and kissed the sun, she could not have felt more aflame.

His kiss became more intense, his tongue tormenting her own, rousing in her the warm sensation of floating in the air.

Then she felt his hands at her neck, releasing her hair. She felt it drift through the air behind her, flowing downward, his fingers moving through the softness.

He drew back his hands, moving up to gently hold the sides of her face, his expression one of awe. "You're breathtaking," he whispered. "You're really beautiful."

His whisper, his voice, struck her soundly, bringing her harshly back into the world of reality. For an instant she stood paralyzed, gazing wide-eyed at him. Her arms dropped like lead weights from around his neck and she glared rigidly at him. Facing him now, she couldn't speak or think. She could only moisten her dry lips and stare.

His masculine voice was unusually deep and shaky when he spoke. "There's so much we've got to learn about each other." He laughed softly. "I didn't mean to offend you."

At his words she felt her professional strength flowing back into her. "And just how do you go about offending someone when you mean to?" she asked sharply.

With a look of surprise his eyes swept her face as they stood facing each other. "I love you," he said, his voice charged with emotion. "A year from now I will love you. Fifty years from now I will love you. In short, I'll always love you."

She hesitated before speaking. "My dear man," she began uncertainly, "a year from now I might believe you *if*," she emphasized, then repeated, "*if* we had developed a relationship that could substantiate those words. And certainly I might believe it after fifty years. But as for now, you don't know me, and certainly no one can speak for always." She spun away from him and walked back to her desk. With her back to him she insisted coolly, "What happened a few minutes ago must be forgotten, completely eliminated from conscious thought."

His voice called from behind her, "Are you going to forget it?" he asked in an almost inaudible voice.

"Most certainly I am," she replied with great assurance.

In the next instant she felt his hands grip her shoulders and he strongly turned her about. "My darling," he said quietly, "you will never forget it, any more than I will. And one other thing before I leave—I want you to know that you're going to love me, whether or not you think you will, or whether or not you want to. I will someday in the future hear those words from your mouth." He lifted her face with one hand, leaned forward, and brushed her lips lightly. "I've got to get across the street, so I suppose this session is over. But I'll see you later." Another quick peck on the lips and he released her and moved quickly toward the door.

Reaching for the doorknob, he suddenly hesitated and asked, his brow rising with his question, "Why do you do this?" He suddenly tapped his teeth with his thumbnail.

Her wide eyes froze on his inquiring face. "I'm sure I don't know what you're talking about, or why it's any concern of yours what I do."

He laughed, turning back to the door. "I think you do it by habit when you're in a situation you're uneasy with, like last night at the beach club. But don't worry, I can help you break the habit. I went throught a stage where I blinked a lot. Like this." He blinked rapidly for a second or two. "But you don't see me blinking now, do you?"

In the next quick move he went through the door, closing it softly behind him. She fell into her chair and her first move was to her teeth with her thumb. She stopped midair and glared at the polished red nail. Annoyed, she dropped the hand back onto the desk.

The next second the door opened and Chandra came in with the next folder. "My goodness, Dr. Lockridge, what happened to your hair?"

Kasha's hand flew to her head, and after a moment she swallowed and whispered, "The pins fell out."

Chandra eyed her for a moment, but said nothing more. But, when she lifted Jeff Bannerman's folder, she smiled.

## CHAPTER FOUR

Chagrined, irritated, annoyed. All described her mood beautifully. She sat behind her desk motionless, her eyes fixed on the file of the departing couple. Apprehension and strain were evident in her face, but no more so on her face than deep inside her. She had never come across a man, patient or otherwise, like Jeffrey Bannerman at any time in her life. But she would settle this thing once and for all. He would not be allowed back into her office, oath or no oath.

She was still quite stunned by her own behavior. Enraged with herself, she knew she could lie if she wished, but truthfully she had to face the obvious. The man interfered with her reasoning power. It had been irrational to kiss him, and a lie to try to convince herself that she had not kissed him. In fact, she had quite enjoyed it. Yesterday he had come roaring into her life and today had set her blood roaring in her ears. What enabled him to do that? She had met handsome, disarming men before, but not in the professional arena. She had not ever kissed a patient, not in this way. She had pecked cheeks and squeezed hands and even embraced a few special persons over the years, but she had never felt she compromised her position in that particular case by doing so. This morning she had compromised her professional self when she kissed him.

Her face tightened to the point of being almost pinched. She felt compromised still. Jeff Bannerman had taken a drink from her deep physical well—but that was it. One drink. One kiss. Now, that she had considered it, she knew it would not happen again. Where he was concerned, the well had just run dry.

Chandra's voice entered the room. "Dr. Wells is on line two, Dr. Lockridge."

Kasha picked up her phone. "Hello, Roman," she said in normal tone.

"Kas, ready for lunch?"

She hesitated. "Uh—no, I think I'll skip today."

He tried to dissuade her. "This is the second day I've been free at twelve; I thought we might celebrate over the veal and peppers at Fords. Maybe I'm beginning a new routine; lunch at a regular time."

She smiled vaguely. "I'm sorry, Roman, but I don't have any appetite today. Maybe next week. Besides, I need to use this time to catch up on notations before the weekend."

He reluctantly agreed. "All right, whatever you say. Anyway, I've been intending to invite you to drive up to Mobile with me Saturday night. I'm speaking at the Regional Mental Health banquet. Care to go?"

She squinched one side of her face. "Sorry again, but I can't. I promised a neighbor of mine we'd eat at the Japanese restaurant in Fort Walton. Maybe next time," she concluded lightly.

"It's a deal," he said, then asked, "Have you heard from your redneck Romeo today?"

Quite stunned, she didn't reply immediately. How unlike Roman to refer to patients in a less than professional manner. Even though the strip of white sand from Pensacola Beach to Panama City was referred to as the Redneck Riviera, she had never personally used the term *redneck* or heard Roman do so. In a spurt of defensiveness, she replied, "I'm afraid I don't understand your question."

He immediately returned in subdued tone, "The young man who forced himself into your office yesterday. I have an opening this afternoon at three if you should hear from him again."

She countered with, "Thank you. If I should hear from him again, I'll tell him."

A second later she hung up the phone. Again, she questioned herself. Why was she protecting Jeff from Roman Wells? Obviously he needed counseling, and even more obvious was the fact she couldn't do it. So why not allow a colleague? Maybe on Monday she would.

Walking into the reception room after the call, she told Chandra to go on to lunch, then closed and locked the outer office door after the young woman left. She was so uneasy with herself she would not remain in the suite with her doors unlocked. She needed this time to think and sort out what had happened in her office earlier.

Taking her time, she moved back into her office and walked over to the large windows overlooking the street. With her lips pursed she watched Chandra disappear around the corner with Roman Wells.

Then she gazed calmly out to the construction site. Suddenly her deep brown irises became fixed on one person who sat propped on the concrete planter, eating a hot dog. Her fingers clenched together tightly as she stared down at him. Even from the distance she could see the perspiration stains darkening on the light khaki shirt across the chest, under the arms, and down the back.

She stood without moving, looking down to where he sat. The bright yellow hat hid his face from her eyes, but his entire body had a look of intensity. From where she watched she could see perfectly proportioned shoulders, broad and muscular, his chest flat and male, his legs well-rounded and strong at the thighs. Her eyes were not at all displeased with him.

Suddenly she realized he was watching for her. His eyes were on the entrance of the Orman Building. The thought upset her, and with an abrupt turn she moved from the window over to her desk. But she could not force herself to sit down.

She moved again to the window, this time to the side, out of sight should he swing his gaze upward. An uncertain smile toyed with her lips. How strange that she was looking at him from the window and he was watching for her at the door.

She placed the end of her right thumb between her teeth and bit down. Then she released it, unconsciously tapping her lower teeth with her nail. Suddenly aware of the tapping sound, she jerked her hand and thrust it into the pocket of her lab coat.

She noticed he was beginning to fidget. His eyes scanned up the front of the building and she drew farther back into the drapes. He stood and stretched his middle. Next he crammed the hot dog wrapper into the milk carton, took a step sideways, and dropped the carton into a wire litter basket near the planter. The emerald green palm threw a shadow across him as he moved on the pavement. However he moved, his gaze remained on the building across from him.

Her smile broadened. She felt vaguely wicked for not eating lunch.

Again his eyes scanned the building upward. Suddenly he walked over to the makeshift building used as an office. When the door closed behind him, she stood wondering what he was doing.

A white pickup with red lettering on the door drove up beside the building and she watched a heavyset man get out and slam the door. Bright red letters below the window proclaimed Bannerman and Son. Her brow crinkled. Jeff was obviously much too young to have a son in the construction business with him, so she deduced quickly that he must be the "son."

At that instant the phone buzzed and she looked around at her desk, undecided whether or not to answer. She was intrigued by her window surveillance and didn't want to be taken away to look up a charge or answer a question about insurance. Finally the buzz won out. Quickly she moved to the desk and lifted the receiver. "Dr. Lockridge," she answered in a fleeting breath.

"Why didn't you eat lunch?" came the unexpected question from Jeff Bannerman.

She looked at the receiver, then spoke. "Is there some law that states I must eat lunch?"

He laughed. "Certainly is—the Bannerman law. I don't get to see you enough at best."

Before he could continue, she heard a deep voice in the background say, "Jeff, I need you to look over these specifications—oops—sorry, didn't see you were on the phone."

Jeff cleared his throat. "It's okay, be right with you." Then into the receiver he said, "Kasha, got to go, but I'll bring you a hot dog in a few minutes. 'Bye."

"No!" she screeched into a dead line. Shaking her head, she dropped the phone. She stood, her fingers braced on the surface of the desk. She wouldn't let him in. No way would she let him into her office with Chandra out. It had taken her until now to recover from his earlier visit, and she just wasn't up to another session with him.

She threw herself into her chair and dissolved into a shapeless blob, realizing she should have accepted Roman's offer of veal and peppers. Looking blankly at the window, she suddenly became aware of the blue sky outside, which had replaced the gray overcast that had followed her to work this morning. Feeling a strange warmness, she wondered when the sun came out. She sat rocking from side to side, touching her upper lip with the tip of her tongue.

Six stories below her in the wooden office building the elder Bannerman folded the blueprint he and his son had been studying on the slanted drafting table behind the scarred desk. He said pleasantly, "Thanks for clearing that up. I'll get these back up to the foreman."

Jeff straightened and slid his hands into the back

pockets of the khaki trousers. "You got a minute, Dad?"

The large body halted in the doorway. "I suppose so."

Jeff squeezed his shoulders together, then began cautiously, "You know most of my cash is in certificates—uh—I was wondering if you might have a few loose dollars floating around just until I can cash a certificate or two."

Preston Bannerman nodded. "I suppose I have a few bucks. That is if your mother hasn't spent it on these wedding preparations." He began taking his wallet from his rear pocket. "How much do you need?"

Jeff swept his teeth with his tongue. "Thirty thousand," he said calmly.

Preston Bannerman's eyes bulged. "Dollars?"

Jeff nodded. "Just for a week or so, Dad. I need it today, otherwise I'd get it from the bank. But you know how they've always got to check and run reports. Even against my own certificates it would take two days. Tomorrow's Saturday, so it would be at least Monday, and I need it by four this afternoon."

Preston rubbed the thinning hair on the top of his head. "Are you in some kind of trouble, son?" he finally asked.

Jeff gave a quick firm shake of his head. "No, nothing more than a little trouble of the heart. I'm doing what you and Mother have wanted to do for years. I'm buying a house. I've found this place at Navarre Beach, but someone else is looking at it too. Whoever gets the money to the realtors by four gets the house. It's exactly the house I want, at the exact location. I can't lose it."

Preston walked back fully inside the door, placing the prints on the desktop. "Isn't that at the far end of Santa Rosa Island? I can't keep all those beaches straight, but I believe that's where we put up those condos a couple of years ago."

"Yes. It's not far from those condos, but it's a house on the Gulf side. It's beautiful. Rustic, a lot of glass and decks, everything I ever wanted in a house."

His father nodded. "Thirty thousand for a house. That is a good deal. Somebody must really be in a bind to sell for that."

Jeff's eyes widened. "Oh, that isn't the price of the house; that's just the down payment. But when I pay that I can go on and move in. The owner's okayed it. The owner's a lawyer—he's done the title search and drawn up the contract and everything. It's all set. I've already called the movers and they're at my apartment now."

"Jeff," said Preston Bannerman worriedly, "I know you're a grown man and able to make your own decisions, but are you sure you're going about this in the right way? Seems to me you might be rushing into a deal that most people would consider a little more closely. Buying a house is a big step, and particularly a house like the one you're thinking of buying."

Jeff inhaled deeply, then said in a melancholy tone, "Dad, I can't wait. Believe me, I just can't."

Preston made a coughing sound, then said, "Well, I want you to tell me that you're not letting what happened years ago make this decision for you. You haven't said, but I know somewhere in all this there's a woman. Apparently a very important one by the fact you haven't asked me for a dime in ten years. Son, believe me, I'm not judging you, but I just want to be sure you're not allowing the past to cloud your mind now. In short, I want you to be sure."

Jeff nodded slowly. "I am sure."

Preston shrugged his shoulders. "Okay. I'll call the bank and have Thomas draw you up a cashier's check."

Jeff smiled appreciatively. "Thanks. I'll get it back to you Monday."

Picking up the blueprints again and turning to the door, his father replied, "Glad I could do it for you. It's been a long time since you asked us for anything. I'll get these prints up to Leland, then I'll come back and make the call."

Jeff joined him at the door and said slyly with a grin, "I'll be out for a few minutes."

Seconds later, walking down the street toward the vending truck, whistling under his breath, he had no illusions about his future, none at all.

When he had left the small frame office at the construction site, Kasha's dark eyes had followed him. She considered a dozen alternatives, but finally decided the least complicated would be merely to accept the food in the brown bag he would have in his hand with a quick thank you, followed by a firm, *No more.* She knew she should not accept even the most token gift from him, but with a full afternoon of appointments facing her she would indulge him this one time merely to maintain a smooth atmosphere.

She unlocked the outer door and opened it. She waited. Finally, the elevator door down the hall slid open and out walked Jeff with his paper bag. Beside him stood Chandra Clemons; behind him stood Roman Wells. The three walked toward her in neat alignment. From a distance Jeff began smiling at her, showing his perfect teeth, his pale blue eyes filling with warmth. Even though she tried not to react in any way, she was positive she blushed. She could feel the unwelcome glow on her cheeks.

"Hi," he called out a few steps away, "got your lunch."

Roman Wells slanted his eyes toward her in astonishment, then the expression quickly became one of puzzlement as he halted dead still.

She smiled uneasily, pulling back from the door. Chandra entered first, followed by Jeff. When she started to shut the door she saw Roman standing motionless, glaring over to her. She smiled bleakly at him before closing it in his face.

Chandra moved to her desk, not taking her eyes from Jeff. "How much do I owe you?" Kasha asked in a voice as normal as possible. Giving Chandra a fleeting glance, she entered her own office.

Jeff followed and closed the door. "Nothing," he said softly. "It's my pleasure."

She accepted the bag from his extended hand. "I want to pay you," she insisted softly.

Alertly watching her face, he gave her a good-natured smile. "All right, if you insist," he whispered, extending one arm and unexpectedly taking the bag from her hand.

She gulped when he reached for her. The next moment she felt his lips brush hers, his strong embrace holding her possessively. With his hands entwined at her lower back, he pulled away the upper portion of his body and looked at her. Cheerily he said, "I'm crazy about you."

Pushing away from him, she said simply, "I rarely agree with the use of that word, but in your particular case, I'm tempted."

He ignored her words. "I've got to get back, otherwise I'd stay here with you while you eat."

She looked at him directly. "I don't want this to happen again. Not ever. I do not accept favors from my patients. It's against my policy." She stared at him impassively. "Do you understand, Jeff?"

His evenly tanned face lost its smile as he listened to her. When she finished, he said, "Of course I understand. I think we can eliminate the doctor/patient relationship. It would be easier for both of us." Then casually walking to the door, he said, "I'll have Miss Clemons close my file, or whatever you do in this situation."

A moment later she stood glaring at the closed door, her head tilted acutely to one side. When Chandra walked in a few minutes later with a file in her hand, Kasha had not moved.

Chandra said, "I understand Mr. Bannerman will not be returning as a patient." She hesitated, then added politely, "Do you want to make a final notation on his record?"

She wanted to shout—scream—or do something

63

totally unexpected. Instead, she calmly reached for the file and took it to her desk where she sat down. There was a long pause before she said, "Thank you," in dismissal to Chandra.

She was closing the file on a man obviously insane. Not knowing what else to do, she reached for the bag, opened it, and took out the hot dog.

## CHAPTER FIVE

She awoke early Saturday morning with a soft moan, yawned, stretched, then her body went slack again. For a few seconds her eyelids fluttered sleepily, then opened as she turned her head on the pillow to look out at the new, radiant morning peering in at her from a narrow opening in the drapes.

Turning on her side, she felt none of the tension she had experienced last night, tension which had drawn her body and mind into a knot. It had been hours before she could unwind enough to close her eyes, but once she slept she did dreamlessly. Now she felt rested. The distance from unbearable tension to complete relaxation could be measured by a good night's sleep.

Yesterday Jeffrey Bannerman had loomed as a gigantic problem in her thoughts; this morning he seemed to be only a very small one. Yesterday she had been exhausted; this morning she was calm and controlled.

Getting up from the bed, she reached for her robe and pulled it on before walking to the large bedroom window facing the Gulf, where she opened the drapes fully, then stood and looked out. Several silver-winged sea gulls circled over the quiet surf, one plunging from the flock to snare a fish in the clear aqua water beyond the foam spreading along the white sand. She watched the dives of the gull, then of another for several minutes. The sea was smooth this morning; gentle waves were breaking along the shore and the June sun was shining brightly. She thought that after she straightened the house and ate breakfast she might go down to the beach and dream a good part of the day away just lazily lying in the sun. She already had a perfect coppery tan from earlier outings and had no fear of blistering or burning beneath the intense rays that would beat down on the snowy sand in the hours ahead.

Before beginning with the housework she dressed in a once-piece strapless bright pink bathing suit, pulled on a faded cotton shirt, then tied her long dark hair at the nape with a narrow ribbon. Barefooted, she walked back into the bedroom, made up the bed, spent several minutes putting scattered items from the past week into their proper places, then straightened the shoes in the closet. She was obsessively neat, but stopped short of being a compulsive. She could tolerate untidiness, but fared much better when everything was in place.

After taking care of the upstairs bedroom and bath, she went down the carpeted steps into the large living room, scanned the orderly room for a moment, then proceeded on into the kitchen where she filled the teapot with water and placed it over a burner. While the water heated she ate a breakfast bar at the table, making sure the crumbs fell on the plastic place mat. Then she took an ashtray from a cabinet drawer and lit a cigarette. Lowering herself into the leather-covered chair, she stretched her long legs out on the linoleum, sat back and enjoyed the cigarette, neatly flicking the ashes into the tray every few seconds.

Rising at the sound of the whistle from the teapot, she switched off the stove. Before she could pour the water the doorbell rang. She opened the door, and standing outside was her neighbor and friend, Betty Lee Taylor. "Good morning," Kasha said pleasantly. "Come on in, I'm making tea."

"Make mine coffee, will you?" Betty Lee sighed, following her into the kitchen. "I haven't had much sleep."

Kasha's brows picked up as she looked inquiringly into the heavy-lidded hazel eyes. "Late date?" she asked casually.

Betty Lee yawned. "That, and, Kasha, did you know the Smythes finally sold their house?"

Kasha shook her head, first pouring water over Betty's instant coffee, then filling her own cup. "No, but I'm not surprised, it's been on the market for a while." Lifting the saucers bearing the cups, she stepped toward the table. Suddenly her eyes widened and she felt a start near the base of her heart. She gave her head one quick shake. *No. It couldn't be. Never.* Setting Betty Lee's coffee on the place mat in front of her, she moved to her seat, sat down, and lowered her cup of tea. "Uh—" She cleared her throat. "You didn't by chance see who bought the house, did you?"

Betty Lee's eyes widened as she stirred sugar into her cup. "That's the reason I didn't get any sleep. I tell you, the end condo can be a definite disadvantage if you carry your mother's genes for nosiness. I peeked out the window till the wee hours of the morning. The new owners moved in last night—moving vans, pickup trucks, carloads of people. I'll bet at least fifteen people came and went."

Kasha turned her lips upside down, saying, "No kidding, must be a large family, huh?" She began to relax inwardly. How foolish it had been to even remotely think he could buy a house the same day he mentioned he was thinking about it. Feeling a bit of relief now to know the Symthe house had been purchased, she knew there was no other for sale in the immediate vicinity. She smiled easily across at Betty Lee. "Did you see any children?"

Betty Lee shook her head, peering over the rim of the cup. "No, just lots of grown-ups. I believe an older couple must have bought it, affluent-looking people driving a Cadillac. The woman seemed to be directing all the traffic in and out of the house. If any of the movers were her children, they were all grown. There were five or six young adults, one was wearing an Air Force uniform."

Kasha laughed softly and pulled her second cigarette from the pack. "You have an eye for the men in blue, don't you?"

Betty Lee also laughed. "He was definitely taken. A pretty blonde was at his side every step he took." She sighed. "It's terrible to live next door to someone and see no more of her than I see of you, Kasha. I'm glad we're taking tonight for ourselves. We can do a lot of catching up." She smiled a warm friendly smile. "Japanese cuisine and female chatter go well together." Suddenly she started to rise. "I'll drive us. Seven okay?"

Kasha nodded. "Seven it is. Must you go so soon? I have more hot water."

Betty Lee held up one hand. "I've got to unpack, wash, iron, then pack again. I leave tomorrow night for Miami for a week. The life of a bank examiner, you know, always on the go."

Kasha laughed with a nod. "Okay, I won't try and talk you out of it. See you tonight."

Several minutes later, after cleaning the kitchen, Kasha gathered a beach towel, suntan oil, and dark glasses, then picked up a couple of magazines on her way out. Moments later she had opened the oversize towel out on the sand, positioned herself comfortably on her stomach, and began to flip through the first magazine, the latest edition of *Ms.* An article on the failure of the E.R.A. caught her attention and she turned the magazine back and began to read with interest. She felt enormously relaxed, the rays of the sun warming the skin of her back and legs.

Suddenly sensing another's presence, she lifted her eyes from the page and looked about her. She was the only person within sight on the secluded stretch of white sand. To the far right, a mile or so down the stretch, she could see several fishermen at the end of the long fishing pier.

She turned her attention back to the article, and did not see the downstairs door of the Smythe house spring open. But the movement on the deck made her glance up briefly. She saw the rear end of a man clad in pale blue swim trunks bending over, apparently extracting a splinter from his foot. She turned her eyes once more to her magazine with the fleeting thought that if he was elderly as Betty Lee indicated, he had certainly taken excellent care of himself judging from the superb tone of the muscles in his back.

She read on. Suddenly her eyes froze on the print. Slowly, very slowly, she rolled them upward to peer out the slit between the top rim of the glasses and her forehead. The elderly man had straightened and turned. She swallowed her gasp. Her lids began to blink wildly with disbelief. It was him!

Her mouth gaped with surprise and a crazy thundering broke loose in her mind. She had never had a premonition before, but she had just experienced one. The moment Betty Lee told her the Smythe house had been sold, the lightning had struck. But she had not believed it. And now it was walking toward her in giant steps, over six feet of powerfully built arms and legs and body. His crop of curly blond hair was blown to one side by the continuous ocean breeze. His wide sensual mouth curled upward in a confident smile. Her eyes were pasted on him. She still could not make her mouth close.

"Good morning," he said in a chipper voice. "This is great, isn't it?"

She merely glared at him. Why did he have to be so incredibly handsome, with such nice bulges, tremendous shoulders, and shapely arms and legs. Her eyes followed him as he approached her beach towel.

In a teasing, joking way he said, "I saw you needed more lotion. I've come to your rescue." Dropping to his knees, he reached for the bottle of oil.

She grabbed the bottle before he could reach it and said, "I can manage my own drying out." She swung up into a sitting position, drawing her legs under her. "What do you think you're doing here anyway? This beach goes with those condominiums." She pointed smoothly to the Spanish-style complex with the black tile roof. "You bought the Smythe house, didn't you?" she said very softly, subdued.

He nodded, his eyes flicking from her face to her body, then back again to her face. "Yes," he said. "It's my dream house, right next door to my dream girl."

She shrugged, then said uneasily, "Well, that's your beach from the corner of your fence to the far side. I don't want you to get the idea just because you've bought that house, just because you've forced yourself into my neighborhood, that it changes things. It doesn't," she concluded firmly.

His blue eyes filled with warmth. "I know you're surprised, Kasha. I expected you to be surprised, but I want you to understand that I'm here to stay. Living close to each other will give us a chance to really get acquainted. I already feel like I've known you forever. But I know you're temporarily objecting to me. I can even understand it, you being what you are. And because you were schooled to be skeptical, I'm going to give you all the time you need." Slowly his arm extended and he lifted the bottle from her hand. "I'm not going to force myself or my feelings upon you." He untwisted the cap and poured a palmful of oil. Edging around to her side, he raised her hair with one hand and with the other began to rub the oil across her upper back. "Your skin is hot," he said lightly. "This should help."

She felt his fingers kneading the flesh of her shoul-

71

ders. She knew it was a mistake to have allowed him to touch her. But she felt willed by the warmth of his palm circling, pressing into her back, felt the weakness grasping her middle. The gentle breeze brought the scent of soap and freshly applied aftershave to her nostrils.

At that moment she felt his hand slide lower, sweeping her rib cage, her spine, caressing the small of her back exposed by the low-cut swimsuit. The ends of his fingers slid beneath the material, and at that moment she felt his mouth on her back, melting against the flesh between her shoulder blades. She straightened with an abrupt jerk and spun the upper part of her body around to see his innocent-eyed grin.

Before she could utter a word, he confessed slyly, "Sorry, I think I got carried away. Your back is like the rest of you—beautiful."

She shook her head, fighting back a tidal wave of new emotions. "This is not going to work, not at all."

"Why not?" he asked in wide-eyed earnestness.

"Because you won't behave yourself," she explained in a soft emphatic tone. "A good neighbor does not go around kissing his neighbor's back. This may sound rude to you, but I would be more comfortable if you moved over to your own beach."

He said back to her very softly, "Before I go"—he reached out and extended the opened bottle of oil to her—"would you mind pouring a little on my back. I might burn on the outside too."

She took the bottle and his hand closed around hers, clutching the bottle. Then with his free hand he lifted her chin and put his mouth softly over hers.

She could taste the coconut-scented oil on his lips as slowly he kissed her. She felt a totally unexpected surge of desire for him flash through her. For the first time ever she felt fright at her own feelings. He was thoroughly desirable, appealing directly to her body.

She felt his hand slide away from hers, still clutching the bottle of oil, and go around her waist, his fingers spreading wide across her back. Her breath caught. His chest pushed into hers and she could feel the golden hairs melting into the tops of her breasts. Now she was trembling.

Almost of its own volition, the hand with the bottle of oil came up and she tilted it, pouring the entire contents on his shoulders. Immediately he drew back and looked at her, startlement widening his eyes. Quite satisfied with herself, she watched the heavy streams of oil darken the light hair across his expanded chest.

Saying nothing, he looked at her, pursing his lips thoughtfully. She couldn't help herself, she giggled. His expression did not change as slowly he rose up from his knees.

Thinking that she had driven a point home, she settled back, the broad smile on her lips relaying her pleasure of the moment. Then in the next instant he had swooped down and bodily lifted her from the towel. She flung long legs in the air and he grabbed her close to him. "Put me down this instant!" she exclaimed.

He gave a savage little turn and began loping in gigantic strides toward the water. She thrust against his chest and slapped him against the shoulders with opened palms. His feet splashed through the foam.

"Don't throw me in the water!" she yelled, alarmed. "I—I'll get salt in my eyes!"

He dashed on out until the waves rolling in wet her buttocks, then holding her still above the water, he whispered triumphantly, "Apologize then, and maybe, just maybe, I'll show some mercy on you."

She lifted her chin defiantly. "I don't owe you an apology. You were trespassing on my beach, not the other way around."

"Is this your sea? I think it is, and I think you need to claim it." Slowly he began to lower her so that the cool water came over the top of her legs.

She grabbed him fiercely around the neck. "If I go, so do you, buster!"

He laughed and the arm beneath her hips dropped away so that she felt her feet lowering onto the sandy bottom, brushing his toes. Bodies glistened in the bright rays of the morning sun as they stood waist-deep in the open sea of blue.

She had never known a man this brazen. His hands held her in a loose embrace, locked at her lower back. She gazed at him through the dark glasses. At that moment she had no idea what she was feeling. There seemed to be a greater sensitivity on his face than she had noticed before. His strength and confidence did not seem so overpowering. He wasn't smiling, nor was she.

Her hands went to his arms and her fingers bit into his flesh. Her slender figure twisted in search of free-dom. "I want you to let me go, Jeff."

A fleeting stunned expression dulled the glittering in his pale irises. "Do you?" he returned softly. Her face became shadowed by his as he swept forward in the water and she felt one leg surrounded by both of his. Her thigh touched his and the coolness of the water vanished. She became acutely aware of his body heating the water, warming her own cool flesh. She didn't like it. She didn't like the way her senses were tingling, or the rapid pace of her heart.

A slight wind blew inland, flattening his golden-blond curls against his forehead. She knew she should free herself, but in that instant her mind danced with visions of making love with him. Although they were uninvited visions, they were strong enough to cause her to cast off her willpower momentarily.

His arms curled around her, drawing her gently against his chest. For seconds her hands dangled beneath the water's surface as if lost with noplace to go, nowhere to cling. That was good. She wasn't responding, she thought, at least not outwardly. Inwardly she was a primordial mess.

Slowly one hand came up and took away her sunglasses. His gaze fastened deeply on hers. The fingers of his hand holding the glasses brushed her cheek. All was silent except for the soft swish of the water sweeping in and out. She wanted to speak but found she could not break the hush that came over the two of them.

Slowly he kissed her. The softness of her body dissolved, feeling the fiery warmth of his lips on hers. She tried to keep her eyes open as both hands came up out of the water to grip his shoulders.

He whispered against her lips, "Do I let you go now?"

"Yes," she said in a murmur against his mouth. "Now."

With a deliberate move his mouth parted softly and very slowly he kissed her neck. Her lips were brushed by thick blond hair, damp from the ocean, still scented by his shampoo, and tousled by the wind. Her words sounded very ragged and uneven to her own ears. "That's quite enough, Jeff. Let me go. Now!" Her fingers plowed into the flesh of his shoulders and she pushed hard.

His lips moved lightly across her skin in the hollow of her throat, then downward. "Now?" he murmured, the tip of his tongue sweeping across the fullness of her upper breasts.

Her breath caught in her lungs and held. Her fingers moved into his golden hair and clutched desperately. She was losing. She stirred in his arms. She had to regain her strength. She would not abandon herself to the virile body of a lunatic.

In a powerful surge he straightened, and when he touched her lips with his she sensed the change of tone, the raw hunger, the desire burning her mouth. At this point she could no longer delude herself, nor could she keep back the response to his touch.

With a slight moan her mouth parted and she returned his kiss, hunger for hunger, desire for desire, flame for flame. Her arms wrapped around his neck as her lips played eagerly with his. She felt his tongue brush her mouth, then sensitively join with hers, and at the same moment his body molded urgently to hers.

The water lessened the barrier of swimsuits and she was suddenly aware that this kiss had run its public course. Weak and trembling, she caught his hand sliding down, exploring her back. "Now," she whispered huskily, tearing herself from him. "It will stop now." She began to splash through the water, leaving him standing waist deep.

He stared after her, his face aglow, his eyes burning. But he did not move.

She was breathless when she walked onto the sand. Breathless and very much displeased with herself. Her eyes quickly swept the condos to see if anyone was standing at the windows watching. Finding no one glancing out, she sighed a long breath of relief.

Quick steps of self-anger compelled her along the sand to her towel and magazines, which she snatched up quickly before heading up to her apartment.

He caught up with her at the first row of seaoats growing tall in the sand. "You forgot your glasses," he said softly.

Her eyes swept over him in one quick glance as she reached out and grabbed the glasses with a fierceness that broke the frame. Angrily she sent the piece of frame she held tumbling through the air into the sand.

With a sigh he leaned over and picked it up. Straightening, he said, "I'll get you a new pair. No need to get upset."

She flushed a crimson red. "What I want from you is for you to leave me alone! Why can't you get that through your thick skull!"

Shaking his head, his lips twisted and he reached over and pulled up a single seaoat.

"Don't do that!" she exclaimed. "It's against the

77

law to disturb the seaoats. They keep the sand from shifting."

He grinned. "Well, if your condo starts floating out into the Gulf, you can always come over and live with me."

She stood eyeing him with disbelief, then turned slowly and started away from him. In the coming days she felt sure one of them would qualify for shock therapy, and at this point she wasn't sure it wouldn't be her.

# CHAPTER SIX

Almost tempted by late afternoon to cancel her dinner with Betty Lee, she decided she really couldn't. It wouldn't be fair to disappoint a friend.

She poured herself a glass of sherry and shook her head with dismay. What an unexpected turn of events. Her emotions were astir as never before. She believed in instant tea and instant coffee, and even instant oatmeal, but not in instant love. She was a cautious, private woman who had always carefully guarded her desires, her passions. She had never given all of herself. She had always held something in reserve, some part not touched by another human being.

Jeffrey Bannerman was a potential enemy to that part of her. She had always been covertly suspicious of the male mind and ego, maybe to the point of being slightly wary, but not indifferent. She respected men as men, and in her life she had been close to a few, but had never sought refuge in any man's arms. She was strong and independent and intended to stay just that way.

Emptying the first, she poured her second glass of sherry, took a sip, then pressed her lips together.

Obviously he was an impulsive man, probably not one to think through a situation. Impulsive people sometimes proved to be reckless and the thought she was the object of an impulse was not in the least comforting.

Walking aimlessly around the living room, she listened consciously to the noises about her. In the distance came the continuous wash of the surf along the shore; much closer were children playing water polo in the pool in the courtyard of the complex. Sounds of old life—and new life; sounds of the constant and the passing. In her short years of existing she was impressed with the magnificence of nature compared to the relative insignificance of man. That was why she chose the sea for her front yard. It pleased her. It consoled her. It made her aware of the fact she wrote the script for her own life and lived it according to her own will. She had no dream to rule the world, but had a horror of the world ruling her. She had a horror of any force ruling her, even her own desire.

Dusk fell and, detaching herself from her thoughts, she went upstairs to run her bath. Allowing plenty of time to dress, she sank down into the warm water, leaning her head against the white ceramic wall. She gazed out into nothingness, her eyes dazed. Why wasn't she amused by Jeff Bannerman? Maybe it was because she wasn't looking at it in the right perspective. Maybe she should not be alarmed by him, but rather, entertained.

She smiled suddenly, thinking she wasn't suspicious or wary of him. She knew full well his intentions, and she had no compunctions about those intentions. But it would not happen as he imagined. She would not allow it.

After drying thoroughly and applying lotion the length of her body, she dressed comfortably in a shiny green poplin skirt and striped blouse, and threw the matching jacket across the foot of her large bed. Then she seated herself on the stool in front of the dressing table, first combing and tying back her hair, then applying base makeup to her face. Next she worked on her eyes. As she used the liner, she wondered what he had done the remainder of the afternoon. She had left him standing on the rise holding a seaoat in his hand.

Smoothing out the blush on her cheeks, she suddenly raised her brows. If for no other reason, she would have thought compulsion would force him to call. Yet, he had not. Bringing the tube of lipstick to her lips, she hesitated, then shrugged. Probably unpacking still. After all, he had only moved in last night. Still, she found herself with an almost irrepressible curiosity to know why he had not contacted her again. Of course, she sighed, how stupid, he wouldn't have a phone. Phones weren't installed in the middle of the night.

Reaching into her jewelry case, she removed a tiny gold sand dollar on a chain, a Christmas present from Commander Dennis Sanders, formerly of the Pensacola Naval Base, but now afloat in the Far East on an aircraft carrier. Dennis had been the inflexible man, a player of games, but she had recognized his games and liked him anyway. There had been times in the past months when she had missed his dark, brooding face. For some reason she wished she could miss him now, but she couldn't. Missing someone was a bit like loving someone, an emotion that could not be forced.

Her head bent forward and she slipped the long chain over it. Actually, that was exactly what Jeff was trying to do—force her into loving him. Nevertheless, his game was a little different from most she had played, so she had to be sure and measure her moves carefully. Thus far she hadn't done too well where he was concerned.

Rising from the stool, she shuffled across in stocking feet to the closet where she slipped into low heels. Excellent timing. The doorbell sounded, she picked up her purse and hurried downstairs.

"Ready?" Betty Lee said when Kasha opened the door.

"You bet. Ready and famished." Kasha laughed. Walking along the path that wound to the rear of the complex and the garages, she looked quickly back over her shoulder to the darkened house of Jeff Bannerman. She noted no automobile was present in the space underneath the two-story house. She turned her head back to the path, silently wondering where he was at this early hour, where he had been since the earlier water escapade.

Fifteen minutes later the two women were seated on tatami mats in a unique dining room of the Nikko Inn at Fort Walton Beach. They were the first to be seated on the bamboo floor of the room housing four tables. Kasha looked around, saying, "We must be early."

Betty Lee laughed easily, then suddenly her face

became serious. "Oh, listen, Kasha, you won't care if a friend of mine joins us later, will you? He's at a wedding rehearsal; his sister's getting married tomorrow. Why don't we have a drink and wait for him before we order. That is, if you don't mind?"

"Of course not," Kasha returned cheerily. "A drink would be fine."

When the beautiful Oriental waitress brought menus to the table, Betty Lee informed her, "We'll have someone joining us later. Would you bring me a typhoon while we wait."

Kasha's eyes widened. She looked at Betty Lee a moment, then across to the young woman awaiting her decision. She deliberated momentarily, not quite as adventurous in spirit as Betty Lee.

"Oh, come on, live dangerously, have a typhoon with me."

"Okay." Kasha smiled with a sigh. "Make it two typhoons."

After the waitress rose to her feet and slipped quietly out the door, Kasha laughed, exclaiming, "Did you read what's in that drink? Three rums and brandy! That's enough to graft our butts to these mats. I think when she comes back we'd better order an appetizer. I've had sherry already. A typhoon might just blow me away."

Betty Lee laughed with delight. "I've always wanted to try one. Why not?"

A second waitress escorted another couple into the room. Facing the door, Kasha's eyes automatically swung up, then she quickly lowered her entire head, her chin almost touching the collar of her blouse as she feigned interest in the menu opened on the table. She had recognized the man immediately as her patient, Brad Shaw. He was embracing a shapely young woman with one arm as they were shown to the table in the far corner behind the one Kasha and Betty Lee occupied.

She heard him laughing softly, saying something to the waitress. Kasha frowned thoughtfully. The woman he embraced clearly was not his wife. Little wonder the counseling was not helping their failing marriage. While his family was trying to overcome the one indiscretion they were aware of, he was dining forty miles from his home with quite obviously another.

Betty Lee leaned forward. "What is it, Kasha?" she whispered with concern.

Kasha gave a quick shake of her head. "Nothing. I just had a bad thought, that's all."

The waitress entered the room a third time, bringing the drinks. Still frowning, Kasha stared at the tall-stemmed glass. She had feared the effort to salvage a workable marriage had been hopeless in the case of the Shaws. After spending hours and hours working to break the barriers between two people who said they wanted to save their union, she felt the last hope sliding away.

Then she did something completely out of character for herself. She turned the upper portion of her body around and she stared at Brad Shaw. She had no idea what made her decide to do so, for what she saw was him whispering in the young woman's ear, then kissing her neck.

*The hell with this,* Kasha thought, watching him playing little kissing games. She was going to stare at him until he saw her. Not that it mattered—his entire family had walked in on one of his extramarital affairs and it hadn't mattered.

Finally, after several passionate kisses, his eyes swept up and locked directly on Kasha's face. For a moment he froze, then suddenly flinched and straightened. His face became a deep dark red. As he swallowed, Kasha turned back around to face Betty Lee.

"What *are* you doing, Kasha?" Betty Lee whispered.

"A little afterhours therapy," she murmured, then paused and raised her glass to her lips.

A moment later the table in the corner was empty again. She had not looked up as Brad Shaw and his date passed swiftly by her table, but from the corner of her eye she had seen a flash of his black socks. Feeling absolutely terrible, she raised the drink to her lips. She had never done anything like that to a patient before. And she didn't know why she'd done it tonight. But it was too late to worry about it now. It was done. Frankly, she felt forced to take a dose of her own advice. *You can't change what's done; you can only try to understand why—and cope.*

She sat for a long silent moment, then inhaled deeply and took another sip from the tremendous glass.

At eight thirty, after looking at her watch, she sighed. "I'm really feeling smashed." She pulled out a cigarette and lit it, noting her hand was still steady.

She managed not to singe her long black lashes. "Do you think we might order? What time is your friend coming?"

"I would think any minute. Rehearsal was at seven."

Kasha rubbed one temple. The restaurant was quiet except for the soft mandolin and flute music filling the air. For the third time she lifted the small towel in the bamboo basket and pressed it to her face. She said factually, "He must be someone you like, Betty Lee." She folded the towel and placed it back in the basket. "I don't know of too many men who would make you put a hold on your chicken teriyaki." She smiled. "Tell me about him."

"Well, actually," Betty Lee began with a short laugh, "I can't tell you much. I haven't known him that long." Her voice lowered. "But I can tell you he's a walking, living, breathing dream. If I were an artist, I would certainly want to paint him—in the nude. But"—she paused dramatically—"being a bank examiner, I'll be satisfied with merely checking out his assets and liabilities. He's got eyes that will hypnotize you. Really, I'm not lying." Her thin brows rose and she laughed again. "I always pictured living next door to a tall, handsome man, and even better, a tall, handsome, *single* man." She clicked her tongue. "And now I am."

Kasha's head jerked up. She struggled for a moment before she managed to say, "Did you say next door?"

Betty Lee nodded with a sigh. "Yes. He bought the Symthe house. His name is Jeff, Jeff Bannerman."

Suddenly she wanted to knock herself in the head. She had sat in this wonderful restaurant for almost two hours, drank too much, and literally starved herself for Betty Lee's new friend—Jeff Bannerman. A grave expression drifted across her features and she said tonelessly, "I'm going to order now."

Before the words had left her mouth, the waitress came into the room with Betty Lee's guest close behind. Kasha, expressionless, looked up at him, as did Betty Lee, but with bright eyes and a happy smile. "Jeff, we were about to give up on you."

He looked directly at Kasha as he spoke. "You wouldn't do that, would you? Give up on me?"

She ignored him, but Betty Lee moved over and patted the mat she had just vacated. "Sit here." She laughed, eyeing him with noticeable fascination.

While he lowered his tall body onto the floor gracefully, Betty Lee questioned him, "How did the rehearsal go?" One hand clutched the arm of his black suit coat.

Turning to Betty Lee, he said cheerfully, "Fine. Tomorrow's the big day." Sitting erect on the mat, his gaze swung back to Kasha.

"Oh," Betty Lee said, "this is Kasha Lockridge. Kasha—"

"We've met," Kasha interrupted bluntly.

"Yes." His voice softened. "The good doctor and I go back a ways."

"Oh?" Betty Lee could not mask her surprise. "I had no idea . . ." Her words trailed off.

"Yes," Jeff went on, his eyes twinkling across with amusement. "Your friend has been helping me through a very important period of my life. As a matter of fact, I've never been so well off."

Flushing, Kasha stared across at him, her eyes glinting, daring him to continue.

He smiled slowly, his eyes shining brightly, holding hers captive. In spite of herself, she felt a warm thrill sweeping through her.

## CHAPTER SEVEN

With the third typhoon of the evening the wheels of her mind slowed, then stopped altogether. The meal of chicken teriyaki and shrimp tempura tasted delicious even though she could no longer differentiate between the chicken and the seafood. She had a strange grin pasted firmly on her lips which even chewing could not take away.

The second drink had brought the silly giggles to Betty Lee and the third one made it a permanent condition.

Jeff Bannerman considered his position. To his left sat a low continuous giggle, across from him sat a grin like none other he had ever seen. He cleared his throat before announcing, "I think it would be best for all concerned if I drive us back to Navarre." He looked at Betty Lee's full face. "I'll bring you back in the morning to get your car."

Staring into his face, Betty Lee giggled. When he looked at Kasha she returned his gaze silently, but with the grin. He shifted his lean body on the mat, then sighed before lapsing into silence.

Betty Lee leaned around and stuck her face directly in front of him. "You know, Jeff, I want to do something I haven't done in a long time." She giggled again.

He eyed her cautiously a moment before venturing hesitantly, "And just what is that, Betty Lee?"

Steadfast in his face, she whispered, "I want to get out my net, my flashlight, and go crabbing." Her head suddenly jerked around to Kasha. "Doesn't that sound like fun, Kasha?"

Kasha, her expression unchanged, agreed with a single nod.

Jeff studied the two a moment, then said under his breath, "Watch out, crabs," as he gestured toward the waitress.

Five minutes later he was maneuvering them both in the direction of his car, Kasha walking erect and stiff, not bending her knees even slightly.

At the passenger door of his sports car an argument ensued when Betty Lee ventured, "I'll get in the back. My legs are shorter than yours, Kasha." She giggled.

Speaking for the first time in thirty minutes, Kasha stepped quickly in front of her, saying, "No, I'll get in the back. I'm thinner." She stepped forward, her arms reaching for the back of the seat, her heel landing on Betty Lee's foot.

An immediate shriek pierced the air. "Oooow, you're on my foot, Kasha!"

Her head already lowered to climb into the car, Kasha suddenly straightened, bumping the back of her head on the metal frame. A loud thud and she fell back from the door, completely addled for an instant.

Finally Jeff stepped forward, grasped one arm of

each woman tightly, and said firmly, "Tell you what, why don't *both* of you get in the backseat, otherwise we'll be here all night." Releasing Betty Lee's arm, he pulled the seat sharply forward and commanded, "In you go."

Betty Lee began climbing awkwardly into the rear seat of the car. During her struggle Jeff brought Kasha around and stared straight into her dark eyes. "Shame on you," he whispered, then added, "What would your partner think if he could see you now?"

She glared back at him indignantly, raising her chin. Then suddenly she leaned close and puckered her lips, kissing the air between them in quick phantom kisses.

He flushed and his brows raised. "Don't tempt me, darling. I don't usually take advantage of a situation like this, but in your case I just might."

"I'm in. I'm in," Betty Lee squealed triumphantly.

As Kasha leaned toward the door, Jeff's hands went firmly to her waist to assist her in. Reaching back, she slapped his hands, saying, "When I need your help, I'll ask for it!"

His fingers clutched tighter into her waist as she continued to strike at him while climbing into the compact seat beside Betty Lee. Releasing her, he pushed the seat back, slammed the door, and walked to his side of the car.

Betty Lee giggled. "We both have a window seat, Kasha." She pressed her nose against the triangle-shaped glass, adding, "But look how small the windows are."

Getting in under the wheel, Jeff looked back at them, then turned his head forward, shaking slowly.

Under his breath he grunted, pulling from the parking lot. "Lucky for you two I made it tonight or the county would have probably housed you till Monday."

Betty Lee's hands caught on his seat and she pulled herself up, straightening her spine. "Oh, no, Jeff," she laughed, "we would have called a cab. It costs twenty dollars cab fare from Fort Walton to Navarre, but I never drive after more than one drink."

He raised one hand slightly from the steering wheel, asking with a hint of surprise, "Do you do this kind of thing often?"

Betty Lee opened her mouth, but Kasha interrupted with the quick reply, "Every week. Sometimes twice if Betty Lee is in town. We love the feeling of freedom associated with it."

When Betty Lee looked over to her strangely, Kasha nudged her into silence, then coaxed her into agreeing with a threatening expression. "Yeah," Betty Lee finally added in a whisper, "freedom."

Jeff glared swiftly into the rearview mirror, then back onto the highway. "Well, you'd better watch your quest for freedom, first thing you know you'll be putting a little 'inspiration' in your morning coffee."

Kasha hesitated a moment, then drawled in low words, "Nothing stronger than a little vodka ever goes in our coffee."

Betty Lee gave her a totally perplexed stare, then inhaled deeply before lapsing into an astute silence.

Jeff's lips twisted thoughtfully and again his eyes swept the mirror, glimpsing the smug expression on the pretty, smooth face. He was silent until he turned from the highway onto the long bridge leading over to the island, and after glancing at the dash clock, said, "It's almost one now; maybe we should hold off on catching crabs tonight."

"Oh," Betty Lee sighed in heavy disappointment. "I had my heart set on it."

"Me too," Kasha joined in dramatically. "Think of all the crabs out there, practically fighting to climb into our nets. Millions of them, I'm sure." During the trip her mind had cleared enough to realize the first thing he would try to do after reaching the island would be to separate her from Betty Lee. If she had one thing, it was Jeffrey Bannerman's number. Spare the crabs and catch her in his net; well, that would be the day he could write Eureka in his diary, an entry she never planned for him to make in her lifetime.

After considering a moment, he said softly, "Well, since you both want to, I guess we can for a little while, but not too late because I do have a wedding to attend tomorrow." He laughed, correcting himself, "Today."

He pulled up and halted behind the condo. "Meet you at the beach in ten minutes."

After finally dislodging herself from the car, Kasha reached in and helped Betty Lee out while Jeff sat unmoving beneath the wheel watching them with a sly grin on his lips directed at Kasha.

When Betty Lee's short legs finally touched the pavement, Kasha shut the car door with a hard slam in his grinning face. Both women started to walk away from the car. Betty Lee took a step, then sud-

93

denly halted abruptly, jerking her head around. "Ka-sha, you shut the door on my skirt!"

Quickly Kasha reached out and opened the door, freeing Betty Lee to parade off without her.

Leaning over the passenger seat, Jeff grinned and winked. "Haste makes waste, darling. If I had driven off, you would be minus a friend, or your friend would be minus a skirt." The door slammed again in his chuckling face.

After her long strides caught up with Betty Lee, he drove off and a second later she saw him pull into the drive of his new house.

Betty Lee sighed softly. "He certainly is a good-looking man, isn't he, Kasha?"

"If that type appeals to you," Kasha replied briefly.

Betty Lee's brows raised in question. "And what type is that?"

"Sex fiend."

Betty Lee nodded wildly, her sudden laughter mingling with the stiff gulf breeze. "It does . . . it does," she said from deep in her throat.

Kasha's eyes widened at her friend and the wheels began to turn, cranking out the most delightful thought. Whoever it was who said Three's a crowd, certainly created a meaningful cliché.

She waited until Betty Lee turned in the direction of her rear door before saying leisurely, "Uh, I'm so tired. I think maybe I'll pass on this beach excursion. You wouldn't mind, would you?"

Betty Lee looked momentarily surprised, then said, "Of course not. I'll even catch one for you."

Walking on to her own complex, Kasha felt the

94

slow smile spread along her lips. That was exactly her intention. A classic solution. Eliminate the third of a threesome, and it left a perfect twosome, alone at the water's edge under a beautiful starlit night. A handsome man, an attractive woman—a better arrangement didn't exist.

She went quietly into her apartment, up the stairs to her bedroom, and slowly undressed. Pulling on her nightgown, she yawned long and wide, thoroughly pleased with herself and her plan. Walking over to the large window, she peered out into the night, her eyes scanning the shimmering white sand. There they were—two flashlights near the edge of the bubbly surf. It didn't require a lot of imagination on her part to know where this particular traipsing through the surf would lead.

She sat down sluggishly on the windowseat, wrapping her arms around her knees. Again she yawned, then her lips relaxed in a sly grin. Less than fifty yards away, Betty Lee plowed through the knee-deep water with a delighted giggle, chasing a swift-moving crab with her net. Of course the angling sea creature escaped, as had all the others she had chased.

Jeff Bannerman, distinctly silent, cut his eyes up to the window. She was still there—watching. The waves swept in rhythmically, then receded in a soft gurgle. A slow, knowing grin began to spread on his mouth. After a few more minutes passed, every few seconds checking the window of the apartment, he commented to Betty Lee, "You know, I think we should give the crabs a rest and turn off the flashlight so we don't run down the batteries." He sighed, then added, "And rest a while ourselves."

Betty Lee looked at him, surprised. "Okay with me." She giggled.

He walked first from the water. "Why don't we just walk over here." He led the way to a high rise in the sand topped with tall seaoats. Then he reached for Betty Lee's flashlight and switched it off. He sat down and patted the sand beside him and Betty Lee obediently lowered herself. Turning around, he craned his neck and saw exactly what he hoped to see. The condo was completely obscured from view. If he couldn't see her, for a fact she couldn't see them, thus ending her peeping-Tom exercise for the night.

Immensely pleased with himself, he said pleasantly, "Have you known Kasha for a long while?"

"About two years, ever since she came here to practice." She laughed with sheer enjoyment, adding, "I was terribly ill at ease with her for a while, you know, her being a psychiatrist, but now I hardly ever think about it."

The next question he considered more cautiously. Cheerily he threw out, "I saw her and her partner at the beach club the other night. Think there's anything going on there?"

Her sparkling eyes widened and a flow of laughter erupted, "Roman? Goodness, no." Then she rattled on, volunteering, "She was going out regularly with a naval commander, but now he's in the Far East."

He glanced around, surprised. "Really? Did she like him a lot?"

Inhaling deeply, Betty Lee responded, "Who can say? You never can tell about Kasha. She's a very private person emotionwise. She's a great conversa-

96

tionalist, but she rarely divulges any information about herself." She looked at him curiously. "Why the questions?"

He grinned. "A guy can never know his analyst too well, do you think?"

She pursed her lips thoughtfully. "You mean she really is your analyst?"

His eyes fastened on the waves rolling in under the bright moonlight. "We've had a session or two," he admitted with a chuckle. "But she discharged me with a prognosis of hopeless."

Betty Lee's eyes widened. "You mean you're incurable!"

He nodded with a wide grin. "Yep. That's what the doctor said."

Inconspicuously scooting a foot or so from him, she whispered, "Think we've rested long enough?"

He sighed. "Let's give it a few more minutes. Who knows, we might just net the biggest mama crab of all times if we're patient."

Betty Lee said a bit anxiously, "I really can't tell a boy crab from a girl crab."

Jeff laughed easily. "You will this one, and that's a fact."

By the time the flashlights went off, Kasha jumped from the window in alarm. Oh, Lord, what had she done to her dearest and best friend? After three typhoons Betty Lee couldn't be held responsible for her actions. She thought this was what she wanted—the two of them to sink down out there in the sand—but it wasn't.

Quickly she slung off her nightgown, pulled on her cut-offs and threw a sweat shirt over her naked breasts without pausing for a bra. Sliding her feet into shapeless sandals, she hurried down the steps. Jerking open the hall closet, she pulled out a net and a flashlight, then slammed from the house.

A minute later she was running through the sand toward the surf. Topping the rise, she slowed, flipped on the light, hesitated, then walked in full control nonchalantly toward the water's edge. She could see them outlined from the corners of her eyes and sighed a relieved breath. She'd arrived in time.

"Kasha!" Betty Lee called out, jumping up from the sand. "Over here!" She dashed out to greet her friend.

Kasha turned and looked at her, saying quietly, "Caught anything?"

"Not yet," Betty Lee admitted with a grin. "Jeff wanted to rest."

Kasha ventured a look at the tall form slowly rising to his feet and said with mocking sarcasm, "I'm sure he did."

Brushing the sand from his pants, he walked up, his eyes twinkling, and said with flippant sureness, "The call of the ocean too much for you, Doctor?"

Ignoring him completely, she turned to Betty Lee. "Come on," she said lightly, "we'll make a contest out of this. The one who catches the least will have to be the cook." Lifting her net from the sand, she headed for the water.

Betty Lee called after her, "Well, I'll be the cook, because I'm going in."

The sudden announcement gave cause for Kasha's head to jerk around. "What!" she exclaimed. "I thought you wanted to catch crabs!"

Betty Lee returned with a yawn and a wave, "I'm just too sleepy. 'Night, Jeff. 'Night, Kasha."

Kasha stood frozen, blinking with disbelief. "Well," she said quickly, "I see no reason for any of us to stay."

Betty Lee turned back, waving a last time. "Nonsense, you two stay. I'll cook whatever you catch. Deal?"

Jeff laughed out. "Deal."

After Betty Lee disappeared through the row of seaoats, he turned and walked directly toward Kasha, a new glint in his eye.

She stood her ground firmly, announcing in a threat, "Unless you want to fit into Betty Lee's cooking pot, you'd better stay a good ten feet from me."

He laughed good-naturedly. "Why, darling, whatever do you mean?" Swinging his net through the air, he moved smoothly again to the water.

She deliberated a moment, then kicked off her sandals and followed him, feeling a new spurt of determination springing to life inside her. If it killed her dead as a hammer, she was going to teach Jeff Bannerman a lesson, one he would be a long time forgetting. If he insisted on pushing himself into her life, she would show him just what such a position would gain him.

With a spurt of enthusiasm she waded into the water, shining her flashlight through the clear water to the sandy bottom. Sighting her first white-shelled creature, she took off after it, maneuvering her net deftly through the water. Bagging it after a short chase, she held the net up and asked impatiently, "Where's the bucket?"

He smiled innocently and shrugged. "What bucket?"

Her eyes blared and her head craned forward, stretching her neck like a swan's. "The bucket to put the crab in!"

Again he shrugged. "I don't guess we brought a bucket."

With sudden despair her arms went limp and she lowered the net back into the water, allowing the happy crab to scurry away. Splashing back toward shore, she exclaimed, "That's it! That's all! Anyone who comes to net crabs without a bucket most definitely has not come to net crabs!"

Sauntering toward her with a careless grin, his brows rose. "Could be you're right."

She eyed him with an uncomfortable glare. "Don't come any closer."

Walking up beside her, he smiled. "Has anyone ever told you what a nice bounce you have in the moonlight?"

She turned on him. "No. Most people I know are more couth than that." Still, in spite of herself, she felt her cheeks warm. Her clothing wet up to her breasts, she realized how the sweat shirt was clinging. Stomping into her sandals and gripping the net tightly in her hand, she proceeded in the direction of her apartment.

He walked beside her. "I'll see that you get in okay."

"I've never had trouble getting in," she returned shortly.

He laughed. "What about a cup of coffee? This wind is cold after a while."

"You certainly may have a cup of coffee, but in your own house, not in mine," she stated flatly.

Again he laughed softly. "Okay, no rush. Now that we're living next door to each other there'll be plenty of time."

She gave him the fish eye but made no reply.

The instant she stepped up to her door, she realized what she had done.

His hand twisted the knob, then he looked searchingly at her. "Key?"

She fell up against the wall, melting into a limp blob of total self-disgust. She had locked herself out of her own home.

His smile widened. "Do you have a window I can climb in?"

She pointed over her head to her upstairs bedroom window.

His eyes scanned straight up. "Well, it's a bit of a challenge to climb in a second-floor window with nothing but a stucco wall to scale." He inhaled with false worry. "Any other suggestions?"

"No. I'll just spend the night with Betty Lee," she muttered, moving toward the next door down from hers.

He caught her arm. "Wait a minute. Why wake up a good friend? I have a spare bedroom."

She rolled her eyes slowly at him. "It's my key I misplaced, not my mind."

"All right, go ahead, wake up poor Betty Lee. I don't think she'll appreciate it."

She rang Betty Lee's doorbell and waited. She rang again. No sound came from inside. She waited a minute, then pounded on the wood with her fist. Still no sound.

"I don't think she heard you. My offer is still open."

Giving the door one more good pounding, she turned and walked slowly down the steps.

He laughed and threw out both hands. "If I so much as touch you, you can have me arrested." He motioned for her to move in the direction of his house.

She thought a moment, then stepped out in front of him. It was near dawn and it certainly seemed she had no choice. In all probability he wouldn't take advantage of this situation. Stepping off in the direction of his house, she returned coolly, "If you do, I will."

His laughter followed behind her.

## CHAPTER EIGHT

She was chilled to the bone by the time she stepped into his house, only to find the air stirring inside was colder than the air outside. From all she could see and feel he had a Casablanca fan in every room, all blades turning at maximum speed. Clutching herself, she shivered while he quickly dashed from room to room flipping off the fans.

Sweeping back into the living room where she stood in the middle of the floor, he smiled and said, "I suppose the first thing we should do is get you into some dry clothes."

She laughed an ill little snort and replied, " *We* will do no such thing. I have been dressing myself for a number of years and I have no intention of altering that habit."

His blue eyes traveled over her from head to toe, then he said, "Tell you what, take a warm shower, I'll lay out some clothes for you on the bed and put on a pot of coffee."

She just didn't have the strength to argue. Sniffing, she went into the bedroom he pointed out and locked herself in the bath. Stripping, she stepped into the shower, and a moment later stood beneath the flow of steaming water. Nothing had ever felt as wonderfully soothing as the hot water flowing over her.

She remained unmoving a full fifteen minutes before reaching for the soap, only to find there was none. Turning off the shower, she stepped out into the misted bathroom and reached for a towel, only to find there wasn't one. Her first thought was, *This is a trap. He coaxed me in here without soap or towel, expecting me to cry out for help.* She scolded herself. *You should have looked before you bared yourself. For goodness' sakes, where's your brain?*

Ending the conversation, she lifted the sweat shirt from the floor and dried off. Soundlessly unlocking the door, she pulled it open very slowly, but only after turning the shower on again full force. Dashing into the bedroom with the sweat shirt as her coverup, she grabbed up the faded denims and long-sleeved pullover shirt, then hurried back into the bath. Again locking the door, she dressed, then reached over and turned off the water again.

Turning the cuffs of the pants up several times, she walked out and over to the mirror. Her lips twisted knowingly upon seeing the full outlines of her breasts clearly revealed through the soft knit material. "Don't you have a sweat shirt?" she called out loudly.

"No," he answered back immediately. "But there are some jackets in the closet if you're still cold."

She was almost tempted to think he had not put out the shirt on purpose, but she wouldn't allow herself to start placing the least bit of trust in his motives.

Taking a navy blue lightweight jacket from the closet, she pulled it on and zipped it up.

His brows arched and he smiled seeing her walk into the kitchen. "You look great," he said, white teeth glimmering at her. He was still dressed in wet trunks and damp body shirt.

"Aren't you going to change out of those wet clothes?" she said caustically.

He smiled over to her, moving from the counter. "I don't disturb you, do I?"

"No more so than any other person with a mental disorder," she said dryly.

His head fell back in laughter, but without a word he walked from the kitchen only to return a minute later wearing a short emerald-green robe.

Unable to decide whether or not he had anything on under the robe, she moved cautiously toward the kitchen bar and sat down on a stool.

"Wouldn't you rather sit at the table, or in the living room? You'd be more comfortable," he said over his shoulder while pouring the coffee.

"No, this is fine," she muttered.

He placed the coffee mugs on the counter, then pulled a stool around, positioning it next to her. When he sat down the robe parted, exposing a good deal of one muscular thigh.

Placing one hand as a blinder to the left of her face, she said matter-of-factly, "Would you mind not being so careless with your clothing. I have no desire to view your anatomy."

He leaped from the stool in a huff and ripped open the robe, revealing tight-fitting running shorts and a low-cut body shirt. He exclaimed in a loud voice,

105

"And I have no desire to reveal my anatomy to you, *Doctor*."

"Good." Her brows rose as she lifted the mug to her lips. "We both agree on something—at last."

He fell back on the stool and leaned forward in a slump over the counter, his face a big sulk. "You know what," he drawled in a whisper, "loving you may not be the easiest thing I ever did."

She nodded. "Then take my advice—and *don't*. When I want love, I'll ask for it."

He looked at her slowly, deliberately, as though he were seeing her for the first time. "I'll bet you don't save many marriages, do you?" he asked, his voice faintly sarcastic. "I'll bet you always side with the woman, whatever the problem."

She looked him directly in the face and said factually, "It is not my job to save marriages. I can only hope to improve communication between the partners involved. And yes, I do find the women to be much more open and direct, and more willing to deal honestly with the problems. Men tend to be evasive and most are perfectly willing to allow the weight of a failed marriage to rest on the shoulders of their spouse. The double standard exists even more today than ever before. What is good for the gander does not apply to the goose." Her eyes widened. "When you marry are you going to have nights out with the boys?"

He shrugged. "I don't know. I haven't given it much thought."

She continued boldly. "And should your wife want a night out with the girls, are you going to understand?"

Again he shrugged. "If that's what you want."

She merely glared at him open-mouthed, then slowly turned her eyes back to the counter and mug. Her sanity was being tested by an ominous person.

He stared at the side of her head. "Kasha," he said very softly, "I came from a home in which my father was the breadwinner and my mother the wife who stayed home and raised the children. There are three of us—two girls and myself. I'm not saying my parents had the perfect marriage; they certainly had their arguments and disagreements, but I am saying they worked it out because they worked at it. They made real attempts to understand the other's feelings and needs. Do you know my mother went back to college after the youngest was in high school. She works in the Pensacola library doing something she loves to do, and not because of financial need, although I'm sure she enjoys that feeling of accomplishment. What I'm trying to say is that my father was as proud of her upon her graduation as he was of me when I graduated from Annapolis, maybe more so because he knew her better and understood her better, and loved her better. There isn't any man alive who loves a woman more than my dad loves my mother."

She looked back at him, wrinkling her brow, avoiding his eyes. "Well, Jeff, every marriage is not like your parents'." She hesitated, then said, "My parents were divorced when I was ten, and each remarried, and instead of two unhappy people, there were four, no five, including me. I've always believed that the breakup of that marriage was not due to a lack of love, but due to the inability to communi-

107

cate." She swallowed hard, suddenly very unhappy with herself for sharing secrets of her life.

"So that's why you're a marriage counselor," he commented very softly.

Somewhat exasperated, she glared at him, making a grimace. "Nothing is ever that cut and dried."

He continued to quiz her. "Why did you become a psychiatrist? Why not a sociologist or psychologist? Why all those years in medical school to finally become a counselor?"

With a faint smile she answered, "Because I didn't decide until I was late into my residency just exactly what I wanted to do with my training. When I finally decided, I entered into the partnership with Roman Wells. I have saved no marriages, but I have been effective in assisting the parties involved in establishing meaningful communication which enables them to decide whether or not the obstacles confronting their marriage can be overcome." She sighed and stated, "Some cannot. But at least when the persons divorce, they know why. And it's important to know why." She leaned toward him the slightest bit and said, "Like you, Jeff. I am a professional and I know your approach to this relationship is not only unorthodox, but motivated by"—she shrugged—"something . . ."

"Hey." He laughed, a bit ill-at-ease. "Is this a house call?"

She stared at him. "Not at all. But I am curious why you have chosen this approach and directed it at someone who has made a life work of—" She stopped mid-sentence, hesitated a moment, then asked factually, "Are you crying out to me for help?"

108

For a moment he merely glared at her, his eyes wide. Then slowly he moistened his lips, the movement of his tongue masking a smile. "And if I should," he half-whispered, "would you hear me?"

Managing a small smile, she said, "I would try."

In that instant he bolted from his stool, clasped her wrist firmly, and pulled her from hers.

Her brown eyes became enormous, momentary surprise preventing her from the slightest exclamation.

He released her arm, caught her face with both hands, leaned close to her mouth, and breathed, "Help."

She stiffened immediately. "That's not what I meant!" She placed her hands on his chest to hold him back.

Pressing his fingers in under her long hair, he held her head immobile. "Help," he repeated in a murmur, drawing closer to her lips, his eyes resting on hers.

She felt her chest tighten and a sudden nervousness gripped her. "Let me go this minute!" She tried to wrestle her head free of his hands, her long hair sweeping the air. "Jeff, you gave me your word," she reminded him hotly.

A sensuous little smile played on his lips as he whispered, "That was before you diagnosed me. Now I'm not responsible." He lifted her face and gently touched her lips with his.

For an instant she couldn't breathe, choked by his closeness. She knew this had to stop, or one of these playful times it would go too far. Even now with his body so close to her own, she found it almost impossible to think a coherent thought. His nearness was far more intoxicating than three typhoons—and far more deadly.

Mustering all her strength, she looked directly into the eyes, feeling the quiver at the corners of her mouth. She managed to say with the utmost firmness, clearly a threat, "Jeff Bannerman, if you do not release me this instant—"

"You'll do what?" he whispered so near she felt his breath sweep her lips and dry them again.

"I don't know." She nodded, her eyes widening. "But I'll do something."

He smiled the warmest, most loving smile before crushing her mouth, then softening and moving his lips over hers again and again. Her hands remained pushing at his chest, but her elbows weakened and folded. With incredible speed his arms went around her, clasping her tightly to him. Very softly he whispered against her lips, "Have you thought of what you're going to do yet?" As he spoke, his fingers caressed her back leisurely from the tops of her hips to the backs of her shoulders.

Very conscious of his movements, she gasped. "You're trying to overwhelm me, and it won't work!"

He smiled, brushing her mouth with his lips. "I'm trying to love you, no work involved."

Maybe it was the residual effect of the typhoons, or maybe it was nothing more than battle fatigue from fighting his advances—in the office, on the beach, now—but for some inexplicable reason a kind of recklessness began to creep into Kasha's mind. Perhaps young, masculine Mr. Bannerman needed a

110

dose of his own medicine. While he tried to work his magic, she had a little trick of her own up her sleeve.

Again he brushed her lips, saying softly, "You are so—"

Before he could finish, her hand ran violently down his chest in search of a patch of soft flesh, which she found at his waist. Grabbing a pinch between her thumb and forefinger, she twisted firmly. His response was instantaneous. His arms flew from around her as he stepped back and began to rub his side, eyes round and glinting with disbelief, his jaw hanging loose. "You pinched the hell out of me!" He did a little dance on his toes and flung his words at her with quick little gestures of one hand. "Why did you do that!" he half-yelled, still rubbing the red spot. "My God!" He jerked his head, slanting his face close to hers. "Was that professional!" Blue eyes bulged. "Do doctors ordinarily pinch!"

Turning back to her stool, she said frankly, "Sometimes we must resort to primitive medicine." She sat down and lifted the mug. "I was trying to get your attention and you weren't listening. So, do I have your attention now?" Turning to look at him, her eyes flickered over his face.

He continued to stare at her, his expression one of total solemnity.

She sipped her coffee, then turned once more to him. "You will not overwhelm me, if you get my meaning," she said softly, then added, "My body does not control my mind, rather the opposite. My mind controls my body. I hope you understand, Jeff."

He took a single step and flopped on the stool

beside her, saying with a half-hearted grunt, "If your heart can pinch like your hands, we're in for a rough time ahead."

She immediately countered with, "That's the point I'm trying to make; there isn't a rough time ahead for us, there is *no* time ahead, not for us."

He looked at her and said, "I don't believe that." He sighed forlornly, then sat in a thoughtful silence before saying, "Maybe all this *is* my fault." Inhaling deeply, he nodded. "I can understand your reservations, but I want you to understand my feelings too. I want us to get to know each other because I think when we do we're going to like what we discover."

"Why don't we begin," she insisted, "with the truth. You're an intelligent man, you know your reasons. Why don't you share them."

He looked at her and said seriously, "Because I don't want you analyzing me."

She toyed with a single strand of her hair before replying. "What do you think I've been doing? Did you not know that from the first moment you walked into my office I have done little else? Some force has propelled you into my life and I want to know what that force happens to be."

"Kasha," he explained, "I did not know you were a psychiatrist until the day I walked into your office. For all I know you could have been any of those other doctors. And if you had been the obstetrician or pediatrician or hematologist, I would have done the same thing. It's the woman, not the professional title I find attractive."

She looked at him without blinking. "Would you mind if I get more coffee?"

Looking back soberly, he said, "Of course not. You may have anything you want."

She smiled. "Good. I would like cream and sugar this time. The typhoons have blown over." She moved confidently from the stool behind the counter and poured her coffee. Glancing over her shoulder, she inquired lightly, "Care for more?"

"Might as well," he replied with a sigh.

Suddenly peering out the window, her eyes widened. "It's daylight."

He nodded.

Walking back to the stool, she suddenly sneezed. Another step and she sneezed a second time. Removing her hand from her mouth and nose, she gave her head a quick little shake. "Excuse me."

After she reseated herself, he said, "Sounds like you're taking a cold."

She shook her head. "No, I rarely have colds." Seeing the look of concern on his face, she added with a smile, "But I do occasionally sneeze." She sipped from the mug, then lowered it quickly, feeling the birth of a new sneeze deep within her chest. With that one she felt like she had ripped her lungs out.

"Kasha, why don't you take a couple of aspirin and go to bed," he suggested.

She shook her head, eyeing him dubiously.

"I won't bother you," he said. "I only have the one bedroom suite, so I'll stretch out on the sofa. I don't have much time anyway before I have to leave for my sister's wedding."

She sat thoughtful a moment, then said, "All right. I think I will. It'll be afternoon before maintenance arrives at the condos. So it'll be afternoon before I

113

can get into my apartment." She left the barstool, her half-filled mug of coffee on the counter, and moved to the doorway.

"There are pajamas in the bottom dresser drawer. Take your pick."

She yawned a soft "Thank you."

Feeling much safer and more secure, she went into the bedroom and changed into soft green cotton pajamas. Bending down to close the drawer, she noticed all the pajamas inside were new, never worn. Probably Christmas presents, she concluded, straightening and moving to the bed.

Unhurried, she turned back the spread and sheet, then climbed on the bed where she sneezed several quick times. Straightening, she pulled the sheet up around her neck and nestled her head against the soft pillow. The bed was as hard as concrete, but the pillow was soft as snow.

She heard the door open, but before a word could emerge from her lips, she saw Jeff holding out a glass of water and a bottle of aspirin. "You forgot these," he stated.

She gave her head a quick little shake. "No. I'm allergic to aspirin. But thanks anyway."

He looked at her a moment, then asked, full of concern, "What do you do when you take a cold?"

Her dark eyes widened. "I'm *not* taking a cold, Jeff. But I do need a blanket if you have one."

"Sure." He moved quickly to the closet, opened it, and removed a soft fleecy blanket from the shelf. Walking to the bed, he spread it over her and as he straightened the corners, said, "I'll have to come in here to get my tux, but I'll try not to wake you."

With a measure of discomfort she watched him walk along the side of the bed, bringing the blanket toward her head. She watched his hands, long, tanned, slender fingers with perfectly groomed short nails. When he tucked it around her neck, she felt the strength of his hands, and in that moment her breath caught, anticipating his good night kiss. But to her surprise he slowly straightened.

"Sweet dreams," he said, then squeezed her shoulder and walked from the room.

For a moment she lay absolutely puzzled. Then she sighed and closed her eyes, feeling a strange mixture of feelings. Turning onto her side, her eyes slowly opened and looked out over the Gulf, the morning water very blue and almost mirror-still, the sky bright and cloudless. Her throat felt scratchy and dry, her nose tingled, and each time she swallowed, her ears popped. She stirred restlessly. Finally, after the longest time, she drifted off into a twilight sleep.

Suddenly, at some time later, she became aware of movement in the room. Her lids parted in tiny slits and she peered out to see him standing immaculately dressed in a dark blue tuxedo, white formal shirt, and a matching blue tie he was struggling to perfect.

With a heavy sigh he squared his broad shoulders and again fingers busied themselves with the tie. She watched him, dazed, suddenly conscious of a growing awareness of him as a man. There was certainly no mistaking that fact.

Standing there in front of the dresser mirror, seething with impatience aimed at himself, he groaned aloud, then muttered, "Damn it."

Her lips were too dry and stiff to smile, but she

115

sensed a smile come to life deep inside her. Raising herself on one elbow, she said in a whisper, "Come here, I'll tie it for you."

His head swung in her direction. "Did I wake you?"

She drew in a shaky breath. "No. I think I woke up to die."

He approached the bed, his expression anxious. "Are you sick?"

She sighed and said bleakly, "I don't know."

"You're a doctor, you should know," he said, sitting down on the side of the bed.

She sniffed and declared, "It's probably nothing."

He tilted his head. "Looks like a cold."

Shaking her head, she swallowed painfully. "Did you take Betty Lee to get her car?" she whispered in a groan.

He nodded. "Around noon. She was a bit hung over, but in much better shape than you."

Sitting up, she reached for his tie, thinking even her fingers felt numb and stiff. She focused her attention on the task at hand until the bow was neatly tied. Then she looked up. That was obviously the wrong thing to do. The most electrifying eyes she had ever seen devoured hers. She tried to look away, but she couldn't make her eyes move.

He spoke softly, in a near whisper. "Even like this, you are so very beautiful."

Her mind was about as well-off as her eyes. She wasn't sure his words were complimentary, but she was sure she was past caring. Her insides were weak and trembling, and when he bent forward she didn't move. When his lips brushed her cheek her first

116

thought was that he would take advantage of a sick person. But the thought fled when his lips touched hers in a kiss that made her want nothing more than to melt into the sheets. A kiss that left her breathless.

His arms went around her, drawing her closer to him. Again he kissed her, his lips soft and caressing, holding the depth of his emotions in careful check. Her arms bent around his neck, her fingers gripping into his thick golden hair. She hesitated just a moment, then all reasoning left in a flurry as her mouth parted and she returned his kiss with an intensity that sent them both reeling.

A near-frantic bolt of excitement grasped her and some irresistible force drew her closer to him. Her heart was pounding. She could hear it and feel it drowning her in warmth. His hands sliding over her breasts, down her side, cut off her breath.

Suddenly she pulled away and stared wide-eyed at him. "Jeff!" she cried out in alarm. "Your wedding!"

He looked at her, his own expression a bit frantic. After the longest time he got up, stood beside the bed, and straightened his clothes. Crossing the room, he stopped at the door and looked back at her, his eyes shadowed. "You won't be here when I return, will you?"

She held his eyes a moment, then slowly shook her head from side to side.

"I didn't think so," he said, then went out and pulled the bedroom door closed behind him.

A second later she heard the kitchen door open, then close. At that sound she fell back limp upon the pillow, glaring at the ceiling. She had to admit for whatever reason, whether she was weak in the body or weak in the head, had he not had a wedding to attend, that kiss would have led into total communication. She had not often given herself excuse to flinch at her own actions, but lying there in his bed, she flinched, then shivered. For the first time she was no longer sure of her exact feelings about him. There was a questionable area right in the middle of her mind. A very questionable area.

## CHAPTER NINE

Mid-afternoon she finally reentered her own home. Mumbling under her breath, she went directly upstairs to bed. On her bedside table she placed a quart of orange juice and every once in a while would sip a cupful. She had a cold. She had not had a cold in ten years or longer. He was ruining her health and her life.

With a spasm of anxiety she drew her legs up under her and sank deeper into her soft mattress. She felt her forehead, wondering to what point her temperature had risen, probably close to delirium. Yes, she was sure of it. She must have been delirious to sink down on that hard bed with him. She wished she had been in her right mind, for now he would probably think she wanted him, when in truth nothing could be further from her well mind.

She could hear the surf picking up outside, growing more intense sweeping the shoreline. She concentrated on that sound until she fell into a deep, feverish sleep.

Monday she drove to work clutching her head. She felt as though she were near death and looked it.

Her eyes were watery and bloodshot, her nose red as an American rose, and she groaned aloud several times during the trip inland to the city.

She reminded herself not to breathe on anybody as she alighted from her car holding a giant box of Kleenex. She completely avoided even a quick glance across the street to the construction site. That building might possibly be dedicated as a monument to her memory before this thing with the Bannerman son was finished.

Entering her suite, Chandra greeted her waving a handful of messages. "Dr. Lockridge, Dr. Wells called, as did Brad Shaw, Lorene Hensley, and Jeff Bannerman."

"What did they want?" she muffled from behind a Kleenex.

Chandra looked up at her. "Dr. Wells didn't say. Mr. Shaw is coming in at nine thirty; he said "emergency." Mrs. Hensley wants to discuss something that happened over the weekend." Suddenly she paused. "Mr. Bannerman, well, he—uh—said he had a miracle cure for your cold." Chandra's smiling eyes rested suspiciously on her employer's face.

Thrusting out her bottom lip, Kasha proceeded on into her office, her head jerking with wild little shakes. She sank into her chair and remained there unmoving until Chandra announced Brad Shaw's arrival. Then she straightened and a cool professional exterior covered her.

Brad Shaw closed the door and quickly slipped into the chair nearest her desk. He shook his head, gazing fearfully at her. "Dr. Lockridge, what you

120

saw at that restaurant—it—it wasn't as it appeared to be."

Her brows rose only slightly and nervously he went on. "That—that woman doesn't mean anything to me." Suddenly he paused and clutched his head. "I don't know why I do those things."

A moment of total silence followed, then Kasha asked softly, "Why do you?"

He shrugged, then shook his head. "I know this is the oldest excuse in the world, but my wife, Alice"— he squinted his eyes—"just doesn't understand me."

She observed him a moment. "And do you understand yourself?"

He looked across quizzically.

She continued. "You just stated you don't know why you do certain things, and then you stated that your wife doesn't understand you. Perhaps you expect too much of her. It's extremely difficult to understand someone who doesn't understand himself. Tell me, Brad, why do *you* think you do certain things?" Looking over at him, she sensed the barrier coming down. And when he began to answer she knew at last that the Shaws would soon enter into a stage of meaningful communication. She had not meant to embarrass him, but if in doing so it had brought him to this point, where he was willing to delve into himself to discuss the source of his own weaknesses and failures, it was well worth it. She wasn't yet optimistic concerning the state of their marriage, but she was optimistic that future counseling sessions would be worthwhile to both. He said he loved his wife and children and maybe, just maybe, he truly did. Time would tell.

121

* * *

Later in the day Roman called to invite her to attend a weekend conference with him in New Orleans. Thinking back over the past weekend, she accepted without the slightest hesitation.

She refused all calls from Jeff, and finally instructed Chandra to tell him if he didn't stop trying to practice medicine without a license she would have him arrested. She avoided him as if he were the walking plague. And by Thursday she felt she would survive even the cold.

Then late Thursday afternoon, after the last appointment, she did something so stupid she couldn't actually believe she had done it. She walked over to her office window and looked out. There he was, directly across from her, high up in the new construction talking to a group of welders and pointing down to a beam. Her expression became one of unguarded concern. She had not before considered the danger of his work. One mere slip of the foot and he would plummet six stories to the concrete below.

She watched as he removed the hardhat long enough to brush across his brow with his shirt sleeve. His golden hair, molded close to his head from the hat, glistened in the sunlight. She caught her lower lip with her teeth, watching his lean, muscular body move gracefully from the beam back onto the elevator. When the elevator began downward, she sighed a long breath and went back to her desk to complete final notations on the last file.

Suddenly she pushed back in her chair and stared into space. He had not tried to contact her since Tuesday. She wondered why. If anything could be said for him since the start, it was that he was persistent. Touching the corner of one eye thoughtfully, she wondered if he had given up. That thought put her in a strange mood.

She sat quietly for the longest time with vague, unclear impressions for company.

That afternoon she walked along the water's edge, the first time since the night she caught cold netting for crabs. Dressed in bright red shorts and a matching red and white striped shirt, she walked almost to the long fishing pier before turning back in the direction of her house.

The breeze was soft and fresh, cooling the blistering rays of the late afternoon sun. She passed a couple of tourists who were leaving the white sand in a genuine parboiled state. The spray of the water at her ankles and the exercise associated with a brisk walk combined to make her legs feel good and strong once more. She had completely recuperated from her cold.

She sat down in the sand below the row of seaoats, wrapped her arms around her legs, rested her chin on her knees, and watched the gentle caress of the bubbly surf lap the beach slowly, then withdraw, only to come rushing back again. She cut her eyes to the west where the sun, burning low in orange and red flames, was beginning to set.

Taking in a deep breath of the magnificent breeze, she rose slowly to her feet and started up the path to her apartment. Before walking inside, she glanced over at the empty driveway leading to the house belonging to Jeff. Pursing her lips thoughtfully, she went quietly in and closed the door gently behind her.

Making herself a cup of tea, she sat down at her table with a magazine. Her eyes ran over the print, but she suddenly realized she wasn't reading. She sat serenely composed, but doing absolutely nothing except thinking about Jeff Bannerman, wondering what prompted the sudden change in him.

She had been sitting at the table for close to fifteen minutes when the phone rang. Quickly she jumped to her feet and ran over to the wall extension, then suddenly slowed, waiting for the second ring before she lifted the receiver and said, "Hello," in a completely normal tone.

"Kasha?"

Hearing Jeff's voice, she almost sighed a breath of relief, but instead said, "Yes."

"This is Jeff."

"Hello, Jeff." She fought back the smile.

"Would you like to go to the outdoor theater tonight?" He talked fast. "That is if you've recovered from your illness and don't think the night air will harm you."

She paused a moment, then said, "I'd like that. And yes, I'm well, and no, I don't think the night air will harm me."

"Great. Will seven thirty be okay?"

"That's fine."

After replacing the receiver, she stood twisting the cord and pondering his tone of voice. Certainly he sounded more subdued than she'd ever imagined he could be.

She went upstairs slowly, bathed and dressed, but all the while something about his voice nagged at her mind. She surmised he was unhappy and predicted before the evening ended she would know why.

She greeted him pleasantly at the door in a a low-cut melon-colored dress with matching wrap.

"You look very pretty," he said softly, but without a smile. Then without another word he extended his hand and together they walked to his car. When he opened the door, he grinned. "Front seat or back?"

Biting her tongue, she looked quickly at him, then slid into the front seat. She watched him a moment through the window. He looked very handsome in brown dress pants, matching tie, and a coat and shirt in a soft beige.

The play began promptly at eight, but the Pensacola Players held her attention far less than the man seated beside her. He sat still as a statue, his lids occasionally blinking, his mouth solemn and set.

It was cool, and she used that excuse at the first intermission to leave before seeing the final two acts. This time when they were seated in the car, she looked over to him and whispered, "Jeff, what's wrong?"

He gave her a brief, strange gaze, then asked, "Would you like something to eat?"

Giving her head a quick shake, she asked, "I would like to know why you're acting so strangely."

He was silent a moment, then said calmly, "You don't care anything about me, do you? I mean, really."

Stunned, she frowned. "I—" She stammered. "I don't know. Why are you asking such a question?"

He looked at her again, then guided the car from

the crowded parking lot. He flipped on the tape player and lapsed into silence.

Not knowing what to say or even think, she turned her gaze to the side window.

Suddenly he lowered the volume of the music and asked softly, not looking in her direction, "Have you ever been married?"

Her dark eyes fixed on his profile. "No."

"Engaged?" he pursued.

Again, the short, "No."

"In love?"

Bewildered, she widened her eyes. She returned the question with a question of her own instead of giving him an answer. "Have you ever been married?"

He shook his head. "No."

"Engaged?"

He hesitated a long while, then grinned over at her. "So that's how you do it, just turn the tables."

It struck her immediately he had avoided answering the question. She put her hand on his arm, pressing into his sleeve and repeated. "Have you ever been engaged, Jeff?"

He said nothing for at least five miles before finally admitting, "Once."

She couldn't clearly see his expression in the dark, but she had the distinct feeling that the answer to his impulsive actions concerning Kasha Lockridge could be traced directly to that "once." "Would you like to talk about it?" she said very softly.

His eyes darted toward her and he asked hoarsely, "Would you like to tell me why you're going to New Orleans with Roman Wells this weekend?"

Her mouth parted with surprise. "How do you know that?"

He raised his voice. "You're not denying it!"

Completely taken aback, she replied, a bit tense, "Should I?"

He did not answer. Instead, he reached over and turned up the volume on the music.

She looked at him sharply. So that's what the long face was all about. Some little bee had flown under his hardhat and buzzed into his hard head the fact she and Roman were going to New Orleans. Jealousy. Well, he could brood from now until the tide stood still and he would not alter her life-style one little bit. Jealousy. She shook her head slowly. She just couldn't believe it.

Still very much flushed when he drove up behind her apartment, she flung open her door and alighted in a near run. His long legs caught up with her at the back door. He said in a quick burst, "I'm not finished with this discussion."

Her eyes grew grotesquely large. "I think maybe you are!" Anger at him was nearly choking her.

They wrestled for the key several moments before he emerged victorious and rammed it into the lock. Flinging open the door, he walked in first, then stood aside for her to enter.

Stepping inside, she eyed him coolly and said, "Get out of my house."

With no expression he looked at her, then with fingers spread wide, pushed the door closed. "It doesn't matter a damn that I love you, does it?" he said accusingly, then answered his own question,

"No, not in the least. If it did, you wouldn't be running off to New Orleans with another man."

Her face flushed with color. "I'm not going to discuss it," she quickly recounted her earlier convictions. "You're exactly as I thought you'd be. Exactly! You'll be one of those charming husbands who does whatever he wants to do, but forbids his wife the slightest pleasure."

"By God, you're right!" he cried. "If you think I'll sit back while my wife runs off with another man for the weekend, you're right, I will forbid it!"

She turned her back, saying flippantly, "Well, lucky for us both I'm not your wife." Almost immediately she realized she should not have turned her back to him. But before she could correct her mistake his arms came around her waist in a tight clasp and his lips burrowed through her hair in a near vicious attack on her neck.

She gulped. "How many times must I tell you, Jeff, this approach will not work."

His lips softened, moving gently over her neck in several quick kisses before he murmured, "I love you, Kasha, and that's the only approach I know." He held her firmly, her back pressed close against his chest and abdomen.

She could feel his warmth, his vibrant body everywhere. Slowly he turned her in his arms and she found herself suddenly paralyzed by his closeness, by her own inability to think. Gazing into his bright blue eyes, she felt the maddening pounding of her heart once more.

Moistening her lips, she whispered, "Jeff . . ." And that was the lone word to escape before his mouth closed over hers in a tender caress that caused the pounding in her chest to heighten.

Her arms crept slowly around his neck, her fingers entwining themselves in his hair as she returned the kiss. Pulling away from her slightly, he studied her face a moment, then crushed her to him with a moan. "I love you, Kasha," he murmured against her lips.

A new kind of excitement began to build as she felt his hands travel from her back down to the swell of her hips, pressing her closer to his firm body. His lips moved downward to her neck, his breath burning into her flesh as his mouth moved slowly across the smooth expanse of her body above the top of her dress.

All her senses had taken flight, leaving her totally helpless to stop the feelings surging through her body, and when he took her hand, leading her toward the stairs, she knew she had discovered true insanity.

On the way up the steps, his arm clasping her tightly, his lips on her face, her neck, her entire life flashed before her eyes—the big country home where she was born and raised, her family, her friends, her classmates, her colleagues, and all the while his closeness filtered down all around her. She'd never imagined desire such as this—a passion that left her half-dazed and hypnotized, as though she were losing the person she had been all her life in a tidal wave, and finding in that wake a new person. And yet, all in all, it was a very beautiful feeling.

Inside her bedroom he tenderly enclosed her in his arms and murmured, "I love you." Then very slowly he unzipped her dress, allowing it to float down around her ankles. Lowering to his knees, he waited for her to step out of the melon-colored material, then he tossed it onto a chair beside the bed. His hands traveled slowly up her legs to her waist, and as they moved back down he brought her panty hose and beige silk panties with them.

No longer able to stand without support, her hands dug into his shoulders, feeling the hardness of his body beneath her fingers. At no time in her life had she ever prepared herself for what she was feeling at this moment.

Rising to his feet, his arms went around her again, his trembling fingers fumbling with the hooks on her bra. As the final barrier of clothing slid from her body, he stepped back, his eyes hungrily devouring her from head to toe. "You're even more beautiful than I dreamed," he said, his voice hoarse and shaky.

Moving back even more, he removed his own clothing while she merely stood and watched him. Then he reached out for her hands. Fingertips touched and lingered in midair for the longest moment before clasping together in a squeeze. Slowly his hands came up her arms to her shoulders, then slid down her back in a beautiful and gentle caress while they still stood separated by a cosmic line in a moment so magical each dared not to cross it.

Then he took the step and gathered her to him, and in that instant she forgot everything she had ever known or ever hoped to learn. There was only Jeff in this new world, and when her breasts pressed against his muscled chest and her legs met his as their bodies molded together, she felt the electricity, the desire, possessing every cell of her body, totally engulfing her.

She closed her eyes and his lips were there, brushing her closed lids. Her mouth trembled, and his lips were there, too, building such a powerful yearning inside her she was numbed by it, and breathless because of it. She needed him, and she wanted him so much, there was nothing else.

Her lips found his throat and she kissed him over and over—his neck, his face, his ears—until he moaned aloud, lifting her in his arms and releasing her onto the softness of the bed.

"I love you, Kasha."

Slowly her eyes opened as his gentle words echoed in her ears. His mouth set up flames along her body, bright flames burning, changing the colors of life itself into a light so dazzling it blinded her.

He kissed her breasts until her body reached a height as fragile as crystal. With deliberate slowness he stretched out over her and his movements became her movements, and her sensations became his sensations, until the crystal shattered in a harmonious burst of ecstasy that left them gasping and shuddering together, his head resting against her head, his body covering hers, his legs entwined with hers.

How long they lay in silence, unmoving, she had no idea. Still clasping her tightly, he breathed, "I love you."

Her fingers began to play at his shoulders and she smiled.

They lay in total quiet a moment longer, then

131

slowly he raised his head and brushed her forehead with his lips. "Do you love me, Kasha?"

When he drew back, her eyes held his and she bit down on her lower lip.

"Well, do you?" he repeated in a hoarse whisper.

She slowly released her lip, swallowed, then said, "How important is it to say those words?"

His eyes widened with shock. "Well, it is important." He moistened his lips quickly, then added, "If you do."

"Why don't we not talk about it just now, Jeff," she said, then swallowed. "We've just shared a very special moment, can't we just leave it at that?"

Completely devastated, he whispered, "No." He shook his head. "I want to know how you feel."

Unable to escape his eyes, his questions, she whispered, "In a word, I feel—complete."

He turned his head almost to his shoulder. "But not love?"

Suddenly fearful of his inquiries, she merely stated, "I would really rather not pursue this discussion any further, Jeff. Really."

Another flash of disbelief filled his eyes and he leaped from the bed. "You aren't going to say it, even though you know you do! And I know why!"

Rising up in the bed, she stared at him.

He yanked on his underwear first, then half-yelled, "It's because you're still planning to go to New Orleans with *him*, aren't you!" Furious steps brought him to the bed and he leaned over in her face. "Aren't you?"

"Yes," she said softly. "I'm going to New Orleans."

132

Jerking up straight, he paraded back to the chair and grabbed up his shirt, pulling it on wrong side out, then yanking it off, straightening it, and pulling it back on. His voice was threateningly low. "Well, then, go." He waved his tie through the air at her. "Hit all the good places with your Errol Flynn lookalike." He pushed his bare feet into his shoes and at the same time he rammed his socks into his pockets. His head bobbed up and down. "But I am telling you one thing right now—don't come back expecting me . . . *me*," he screeched, "to make you feel *complete!*"

She inhaled a sharp breath, slinging the covers back and jumping to the floor. She yelled out, crossing the floor. "You—you expect me to say I love you? Well, let me tell you one thing, love is actions, not words. Love is what you *do*, not what you *say.*"

At the door he stood a moment, looking back at her. "Could it be it's both, actions and words?" He suddenly shook his head, a drained expression filling his eyes. "Ah, what's the use," he half-whispered. "I should have known it would turn out this way when I fell in love with a psychiatrist."

"Jeff," she said softly, "you didn't fall in love with a psychiatrist, you just decided to own one, and, darling, you picked the wrong one."

Without another word he straightened his shoulders and left.

# CHAPTER TEN

"I should have known better. I should have been smarter." She sat naked on the side of the bed, nervously tapping her thumbnail against her lower teeth, enumerating what she should have done, instead of what she did. She knew it would happen from the moment she reached out and tied his silly bow tie. Muttering under her breath, she knew she should have tied it a lot tighter. Well, one fact remained clearer than all the others—it most definitely would not happen again.

She struck her teeth with one last vehement tap and fell over sideways onto her bed. She knew the Jeffrey Bannermans of this world. How many had paraded into her office and leveled accusations at some innocent wife who had worked all day and cooked his meals and kept his children, then settled down in front of a television to watch a continuous parade of commercials telling how choosy she must be about some damned peanut butter? And how the last time her dream man had been with her he had used her for a tablecloth, dripping chocolate ice cream and soy sauce all over her stupid white blouse? And then the one she really loved, that wonder man sitting in a lawn chair handed his poor spouse back his shirt because it didn't smell like roses and wasn't as soft as his brain. Well, it was lucky for that man he wasn't handing the shirt back to her, because where she would put it most definitely would not be back in the washer, and it would probably never again smell like roses.

Suddenly she was just heartsick over the state of women in general and herself in particular. She clenched her teeth, swearing silently she would not fall in love with him. She simply would not allow it to happen. She inhaled long and deep.

Then abruptly her thoughts turned to his comments about Roman Wells. Errol Flynn lookalike. Strange, but she had never noticed the resemblance, and thinking about it, she still didn't. But who could say, maybe there waited a swashbuckling time in the Southern capital of romance and adventure. She would be sure to take a closer look at Roman tomorrow.

As for Mr. Jeff "chauvinist" Bannerman, he could live next door to her until his magnificent house caved in from sea rot before she would again be susceptible to his many charms. He was not about to tell Kasha Lockridge what she could do, or where she could do it, or who she could do it with. And he might as well get that fact through his beautiful thick skull. If New Orleans was standing this weekend, she would be there, and she would be there with Roman Wells.

She flipped over on her other side and stared at the wall. If she allowed herself, she could feel hurt over this situation with Jeff, but she wouldn't allow it. She would not allow him to bring pain into her life, not in the name of love. He would have to pick himself a woman with a different definition of that strange little four-letter word.

Drawing the sheet up around her neck, she stared blankly at the wall. Colds had their advantage; had her nose still been stuffy and numb, she would have been unable to smell his scent still lingering all around her. The spicy, tingling fragrance of his after-shave on her pillow, the sweetness of his breath. She could taste him on her lips.

Abruptly she flung the covers back, jumped up, and stripped her bed, then showered, thinking of a patient she had treated during her med-school days who had aspirated a breath mint while making love.

Walking back into her room, she sprayed the air with a medicinal-smelling disinfectant, put on clean linens, and crawled back into bed. Again staring into the dark, every reminder of him was gone with the exception of the crazy little hammering of her heart. And that lingered simply because she didn't know what to do about it. She wasn't up to a heart transplant.


Next door Jeff lay in a lifeless blob sprawled across his postered bed. He groaned aloud. She loved him. He knew she loved him. She could rationalize from now until forever passed and it would not change the fact that she did.

He groaned again and lifted himself stiffly from the bed and went into the kitchen to get himself a beer, his head shaking from side to side in complete despair. This new breed of women—why did they have to happen to his generation? It was impossible to please one of them. If you were kind and considerate, they labeled you "wimp." And if you exerted the least bit of forcefulness, they called you "brute" or "chauvinist." Maybe what they wanted was a brute with wimp tendencies.

He raked one hand through his hair and sat down at the counter, his face long and pensive, his gaze dull. He wished he had eaten Tony's hot dogs Tuesday instead of letting his father talk him into a cooked meal. Hot dogs were so uncomplicated. That hot meal had messed up his whole life. In the booth next to where he sat he had overheard the highly educated Roman Wells telling another doctor friend about the upcoming weekend in New Orleans. Of course he hadn't paid particular attention until Kasha's name had flowed into the conversation. He had nearly choked to death on that bite of country-fried steak when he heard the other man say, "You mean Kasha Lockridge is going with you?"

And it wasn't even what Roman Wells said that was so infuriating, it was the way he said it, so low and sure, with a hidden laugh. "Yes, at last."

His shoulders slumped deeper and he said aloud, "And now you're going, and there's nothing I can do to stop it. You're going off with that degenerate shrink who said, 'At last.' " The corners of his mouth drooped and he repeated again, deep-voiced, "At last."

His fingers gripped his hair, thinking of what would happen to her if she drank a hurricane at Pat O'Brien's. She had already shown her finesse for drinking. His head went up and down in several quick unconscious nods. Yes, she would order one. Anyone who would drink three typhoons wouldn't hesitate to face a hurricane. And from there she would find herself caught in the arms of a moustached whirlwind. From that point the picture became nightmarish.

He hit his knee with his fist. If she thought . . . if Roman Wells thought that he, Jeff Bannerman, would allow *that* to happen, he would announce to the world there wouldn't be a single building left in the city of New Orleans before he did. His job in life was to erect buildings, but he could tear down a few if necessary. A quiet little gleam came into his eyes and he sat motionless for a few minutes before lifting the can of beer to his lips again.

The next morning he saw her whisk to her car as if nothing out of the ordinary had taken place in her life the night before. Well, she could pretend all she wanted, but it *had* taken place and he knew it and she knew it. So just let her drive off in a flurry as though it hadn't.

A few minutes later he drove off down the highway behind her, whistling under his breath.

Mid-morning during a break in Kasha's schedule, Chandra announced over the office intercom in a low voice of dismay, "Mr. Bannerman is out here, Dr. Lockridge."

Leaning forward, Kasha said threateningly, "Well, tell Mr. Bannerman I don't have time—"

But before she could finish, the door opened swiftly with him stepping rapidly inside, Chandra close on his heels. Looking over to her, he grinned his most perfect grin.

She got up from her chair, her brows raised. "Chandra, call Security," she said in a smooth, controlled tone.

Jeff reached out and caught Chandra's arm. "No need to do that, Chandra, this won't take long. And you can be the witness." Again he cut his grin over to her, his blue eyes twinkling. "I only came to apologize for last night. I realize what you must think of me and I want to correct that terrible image I must have left with you in your b—"

"Chandra," she all but yelled, her face reddening. It was a moment before she said in a controlled tone, "I suppose you do need to get back to your work." Her eyes blared at him, daring him to so much as grunt.

Chandra just stood there a moment, her eyes moving from one to the other, and following a sigh, she backed from the room and pulled the door closed with her exit.

All the tendons in her neck tensed as Kasha screeched in a whisper, "What do you mean coming in here and giving my receptionist—" Suddenly she found herself too flustered to continue.

"Darling," he said softly, "I came to tell you I was wrong. I should not have done what I did."

"I certainly agree, and that goes for *everything* you did."

He started moving toward her. "Oh, I'm not talking about loving you, that I will never apologize for, because I do love you, Kasha." His eyes met hers in an even gaze. "But I was wrong about the other." He smiled bleakly and clarified. "The excursion to New Orleans. I had no right to force my opinion on you concerning your plans for the weekend." He clapped his hands together softly. "It's your life, and I know you must live it according to your own strict guidelines."

She stared at him suspiciously, now almost certain he did indeed possess a split personality. She finally drew herself up straight and breathed low. "I will accept your apology." But to herself, she said, *You aren't fooling me. I know a case of acute scrambled brains when I see one.* Still, she managed a hint of a smile. "Is that all?" she said in a professional voice, with a slight tilt of her dark head.

Her eyes widened as his lean frame came lightfooted toward her. When would she ever learn it didn't take much to set him off? It was useless to say *Don't,* because she was already in his arms. The simplest, least complicated approach was merely to allow this kiss, then continue on with her workday.

His face leaned close to her and he whispered, "You've made me crazy."

Her chin raised. "Don't blame that on me."

His arms tightened around her body and the touch of his lips silenced her thoughts. She didn't intend to kiss him. She never intended to kiss him again. She felt the tremble sweep her body and her lips were suddenly hot and wild, crashing against his in near savagery, bringing back all the feeling she experienced with him in the darkness.

His hands were large and fiery, sliding over her back, her sides, wrinkling her smooth white coat. Her lips parted and she felt the sure sweep of his tongue touching hers, stirring and swirling the deepest of emotions, bringing them to the surface.

His hands gripped her waist, pinning her against his body while his mouth moved over hers again and again, kissing her until the excitement became such he abruptly let her go and stepped back, his breath coming fast and short.

She stood looking at him, her gaze completely expressionless. After swallowing several times, she whispered in shaky words, "Is that all?"

Very slowly he nodded. Another minute passed before he turned toward the door. Looking around at her, he said, "How about dinner tonight?"

"I have to pack," she whispered.

A strained little grimace almost appeared, but he fought it back and said, "You can do that after dinner, can't you?"

She nodded. "Yes, I suppose so."

When the door closed, she felt herself sway and then reached out and braced her hand on the corner of her desk. She was still standing there when Chandra walked in with a file in her hand.

Placing the folder on the desk, the receptionist said casually, "You have some pressed jackets in the closet." Then with a wicked little smile, added, "The laundry made a mess of that one," before she let herself out again.

Moving numbly to the closet, Kasha changed coats, then seated herself behind the desk, applied a fresh layer of lip gloss, then calmly pressed the intercom button. "Please send the Shaws in."

When she straightened in her chair, she thought, dismayed, *I'm an animal. That's what men like Jeff*

*Bannerman do to perfectly sane women—make animals of them.*

After the last appointment of the day Roman Wells dropped by to complete the plans for the weekend. He sat down on the sofa and looked at her, his thin lips curved in a relaxed smile. "I'll pick you up at seven. It's several hours over and I want to be sure to arrive in time to hear Dr. Beatty's welcome speech."

She nodded with a bit of a condescending smile. Then her eyes widened. "Uh—listen, why don't I just meet you here. I can leave my car in the parking lot and that way it'll save a few minutes."

He waved off the suggestion. "Not necessary. I'll merely swing across the bridge and hit Highway Ninety, a straight shoot into New Orleans. Besides, it wouldn't be wise to leave your car here; there's no attendant on Sunday." Suddenly his smile changed into an outright grin. "You know, Kasha, I was just wondering before I came over here, whatever happened to your kook?"

A mild blush leaped to her cheeks and she looked at him with utmost innocence. "Who? Oh." She gave a short easy laugh and shook her head. "I don't know," she said, her expression sobering quickly.

Roman also laughed easily. "Well, I can understand his abnormal attraction to you. You most certainly are an attractive woman. I think maybe this time is what we need to appreciate each other in a new light." Gesturing with one hand, he went on lightly. "I mean, Pensacola is a great place to live and work, and certainly our suites here in this building are more than adequate for our practices, but I have been under the impression for a while now that we don't know each other to the extent we should to share such common interests." He paused, then concluded with, "It's been a while since I spent time with a woman who also appealed to my mind."

Her dark eyes suddenly narrowed. Nothing about his declaration bothered her except that little word—*also*. She thought a moment before saying, "I would imagine we'll be able to sandwich some conversation in between the various programs scheduled."

He smiled and rose to his feet, saying brightly, "See you at seven." Reaching for the door, he added back over his shoulder, "By the way, we have the best possible accommodations. Our rooms adjoin, so we can have some late-night wine together."

After he was gone she sat looking at the closed door, wondering how Jeff Bannerman knew Roman's motives before she did. Now she was caught. If she did not go, Jeff would always believe it was because of his jealous ultimatums. And if she did go, she knew she would see the side to Roman Wells she had not ever anticipated seeing, had not longed to see, and certainly would not welcome seeing. Late-night wine sessions with him were definitely out of the question. And she wondered where in the world Jeff ever came up with the idea he resembled Errol Flynn. He looked a lot like Count Dracula, except with a moustache. But then maybe Count Dracula did have a moustache; she just didn't remember. She only knew for sure the latest one sported a thin one. But this one would not be biting her neck.

She sighed heavily, unable to understand what had happened to her beautiful, smooth life. In spite of the fact she had spent most of her life in school, she had never been able to comprehend the workings of a man's mind and she doubted now her ability would improve. In fact, she didn't even want to understand them.

For an instant she considered turning off her light and sitting in her office all night. Squeezing her mouth into a tight firm line, she slowly got up from her chair, took off the lab coat, picked up her purse, and left.

Outside, on the way to the parking lot, she thought, *Maybe I should change my cologne, this latest brand is working too well.*

On the drive home she made a decision. She was finished with men in her personal life.

## CHAPTER ELEVEN

After considering her latest resolution for a few miles along the beach highway, she closed one eye in a squint and tacked on the addendum. *After tonight.*

A faint sinister smile spread across her lips while the thought of the blond-haired builder flitted through her mind. She felt sure his mother and sisters were all charming women, and ladies in the real sense of the word, but she had the distinct feeling he didn't have the true picture of his latest conquest. And it was her intention to correct his perception—tonight.

Hurrying into her house, she glanced over to his drive and her smile widened at the sight of his small silver sports car.

Dropping her purse on the kitchen table with a thud, she passed through, eyes straight ahead, turned abruptly, and clipped up the steps. Turning on her bath water full force, she knelt down, peering into the cabinet and took out an unopened bottle of jasmine bath oil, one of the many bath ingredients presented to her at Christmas by her patients. Suddenly tilting her head, she wondered why patients were almost compelled, it seemed, to give her such personal items as perfumes and bath oils. Pursing her lips, she considered the possibility of there being something there she had overlooked. Wrinkling her brow, she decided if it was, she would have to look for it some other time.

Twisting the cap from the bottle, she passed it under her nose a quick time or two. Whew. She wrinkled her entire face. So that's how jasmine smelled. Holding the bottle over the tub, she allowed all the contents to pour in under the heavy stream of water.

As soon as she was settled in the tub, the phone rang. She reached to the side of the tub to pull herself up and found the enamel so slick, plus the fact she was so slippery and coated with the oil, she almost broke her neck getting out of the tub.

"Kasha," Jeff said spritely as she lifted the bathroom extension, "I was wondering about your choice of restaurants for tonight?"

"Well," she said sweetly, "I was thinking the beach club would be nice. It's so romantic. And"—she clicked her tongue—"we've never been there together."

He gave a short little laugh. "There's a lot of places we've never been together, but I was thinking it would be nice if we grilled hamburgers or something here at my house."

"Oh," she sighed, disappointed.

"But," he said quickly, "the beach club will be great. I'll pick you up at seven thirty again. It'll give us time to have a before-dinner *cup of coffee.*"

When she slid back into the tub, she nodded her head up and down. Wasn't he sneaky? Trying to tell a thirty-one-year-old woman she could not have a martini before dinner. Of all the men she had known in her life, Jeff Bannerman was classic. He was the epitome of the modern male, and the reason why women suffered incurable mental disorders. He had so much to offer, and so many strings attached when he did. Well, he was soon to learn she had just as much to offer, but without strings.

When she finally finished her soak, she couldn't risk standing up in the slimy tub to shower, so she merely stepped out, dried off, and washed her hair in the sink. Her skin was glistening soft and she smelled like a full-blossomed jasmine.

She turbaned her wet hair in a towel, then went into her bedroom where she went through the age-old ritual of polishing fingernails and toenails with the utmost care, selecting a dark purplish-red. Turning on the hair dryer, she dried the polish, then turned the airflow to her head, drying her long dark hair in a lusty style befitting a vamp. She pulled on a deep-red dress which fit to perfection, snug at the waist, tight at the hips, and low cut to reveal a teasing portion of her well-endowed chest. She checked the length in the closet mirror, then turned to the artistic endeavor of applying just the right amount of make-up, finishing with lipstick to match the dress.

At seven twenty-five she sprayed herself generously with her latest aphrodisiac, the one that had caused all this in the first place. But she would be sure not to take it to New Orleans tomorrow. She was willing to play games with Jeff Bannerman. She was not willing to play games with Roman Wells.

The doorbell sounded promptly at seven thirty

and she opened it with a demure smile on her lips in greeting.

He stood handsomely dressed in a black suit, a smile of anticipation on his lips. At seeing her the smile remained fixed, but he suddenly stopped blinking. After a moment he said, "Kasha, is that you?"

"Oh, Jeff." She laughed cheerfully. "After all we've been to each other, don't stand out there and pretend you don't know me."

He shifted on his feet. "You look a little different," he stammered, "I—I guess it's the hair."

She gave an airy flip at one side of her puffed-out creation. "Do you like it?" she asked, stepping forward while he reached behind her to pull the door closed.

They took a few steps in the direction of his car before he answered. "Just don't let a meteorologist see you, or he'll send you up as a weather balloon."

She jerked her head toward him with a mockingly wounded expression in her dark eyes. "Why, I don't believe you don't like it, and when I think of all the time I spent, just for you. And now you don't even like it."

He cleared his throat. "It's not that I don't like it, Kasha, I just don't know whether we can get it all in my little car or not." He suddenly twisted his head at her, adding, "But why don't you keep it over the weekend, I don't want to be the only one to enjoy it."

She was suddenly very serious, the smile fading entirely from her lips. "Now, Jeff, we aren't going to talk about the weekend, or the trip. Agreed?"

He sighed. "Fine with me. I never wanted to talk about it in the first place."

She studied him a moment with a quizzical expression on her face. "You never did say how you found out I would be going in the first place."

He shrugged. "A sea gull flew into my ear. I thought we weren't going to talk about it."

She grunted under her breath, "We're not." And at the same time thought, *I'll bet that sea gull thought he was flying through the Lincoln Tunnel.*

Once they were enclosed in the car, he sat motionless a long minute. Finally turning the ignition, he shook his head and muttered, "I knew there was one more extra I should have had in this car—oxygen."

She smiled. The little car with its neat little bucket seats was so cozy. She said smartly, "If you're inferring my cologne is too much for you, we can always lower the windows."

He rolled enormous blue eyes at her. "What—and risk running over your hair!" His lips twisted, then relaxed as he said, "My lungs will adjust, just don't worry about it. But we will need to sit outside on the terrace when we reach the club."

After he had pulled out onto the highway, she inhaled a deep breath and her left hand fell limp across his right leg, her fingers resting on the inner part of his thigh.

"Kasha," he said in a monotone, "please don't practice primitive medicine on me while I'm driving."

For a brief moment touching his leg, she almost forgot her game plan, but quickly recovered, squeezing his flesh in a soft pinch and saying with a laugh, "I'm only resting my hand."

Without diverting his eyes from the road, he

149

reached and pulled down an armrest between the two seats, then said, "Rest it there."

Dark eyes twinkling with devilment, she made little snail tracks right up the front of his pants with her fingertips, then dropped her arm limp on the padded rest. "Jeff," she said with mocking concern, "I believe you are inhibited."

He inhaled deeply, giving her a fleeting glance from the corners of his eyes. "I thought you wanted to dine at the beach club," he breathed.

"Oh, I do," she replied quickly.

"Well, believe me," he spoke through his teeth, "doing things like you just did is putting your meal in jeopardy." He squeezed the steering wheel tighter and added in a near whisper, "I have never met a woman like you, not in my whole life."

She studied his striking profile a long moment before saying, "Would you care to elaborate on that statement?"

"And have you analyze me? I certainly would not." He shook his head. "I thought those four years I spent in the Coast Guard had taught me something, but in retrospect, I don't think I learned much."

Still smiling at him, she said, "You were in the Coast Guard?"

He nodded.

"What did you do?" she pursued.

He cut her a quick grin. "We guarded the coast."

Losing her smile, she turned her eyes to the road ahead and muttered huffily, "Don't tell me anything about yourself; I don't want to know anyway."

Before an argument could ensue he turned into the drive leading down to the beach club. Stepping onto the sidewalk from the parking lot, he suddenly reached out and caught her arm, saying bluntly, "I want to smell your breath."

She glared at him in wide-eyed astonishment. "What!"

"You heard me. I know anyone who smells like you do is bound to be covering up something. Have you been drinking?"

"I most certainly have not! And if I had, it would not be any of your concern."

He pressed on. "If you have nothing to hide, then you won't mind my own little sobriety test, will you?" He bent over quickly close to her face and commanded, "Breathe."

Flushing the color of her dress, her eyes blared as immediately her head sprang forward and her mouth clamped down on the end of his nose.

He jerked his head away. "You bit my damn nose!" he said somewhat helplessly, rubbing the tip of his nose with two fingers.

"A little test of my own," she stated matter-of-factly. "I call it testing for reflex. And you passed."

He looked at her oddly for a full minute, then half whispered, "What are you doing, Kasha? Why are you dressed like this? Why do you smell like this?" He shook his head. "I—I don't understand any of it."

She replied softly, "Jeff, you have this preconceived idea of what a woman should be, and you might say I'm trying to shatter that idea."

He sighed. "You mean you did all this to do that?" He inhaled long and deeply. "I hate to tell you, but you have already shattered any preconception I might have had relating to women. And I'm not admitting that I had one, but if I did have, it's gone. But by the same token I have always believed that people in your profession, people who delved into other peoples' brains and thoughts and behavior, come away a bit unusual, and you've affirmed that belief. I think it's a hazard of your trade."

Her eyes rose questioningly. "Jeff, are you inferring that I'm not a completely normal, well-rounded person?"

He grinned. "In places you are very well-rounded."

Her eyes grew grotesquely large and she leaned forward in his face. "See!" she spewed. "That's exactly the point I'm trying to convey! You see me as breasts, and hips, and—and—other parts! If you say you love me, you are referring to the objects you see—the body! And there is more to me than a body."

Slowly he reached out and put his hands on her shoulders. He looked at her, then said, "I love your screwy little brain too." His head turned slightly. "I don't understand it, but I love it."

She glared at him mutely, looking into his light blue eyes, and after the longest time suggested in a whisper, "Why don't we just go eat?"

He gave her a crooked smile, reached out and took her arm, and together they walked into the club.

Seated out on the terrace, the soft ocean breeze tousled his hair. He sat opposite her with a strange little smile on his face. Even when she ordered the martini, the smile did not leave. He just sat there, his eyes glinting, his lips curved in a most unusual smile.

It made her nervous. He made her nervous. She sat there clutching her drink, watching him cautiously from under long black lashes.

Following a scrumptious meal she hardly touched, he asked her, "Would you care to dance?"

"I suppose so," she answered, at a complete loss to understand her own feelings. Though the breeze sweeping over the terrace was fresh and cool, she felt like a volcano inside.

At the edge of the dance floor he caught hold of her firmly and pulled her to him. She felt her knees go weak. When his fingers tightened at her waist, she murmured, "Not too tightly, Jeff." But she thought at the same time, *I should not have eaten those oysters.*

It was almost impossible to draw a deep breath, and when he slid both arms around her, she felt a hammering in her chest louder than the drums on the orchestra stand. The music was soft, melodic, and gracefully he moved her in her near-unconscious state on the smooth-surfaced floor. There were clothes between them, but she couldn't feel them. She felt nearly strangled by him and the warmth of his body pressing so close to hers.

He said something to her, but she did not hear it. Pulling back, she peered into his face. "What did you say?"

He brushed her lips swiftly and repeated in a whisper, "I said, let's go."

She nodded.

In the car on the way back to her home, she looked over to him and asked herself, *What is it about this man? Is it because he is handsome; a good-looking face with interesting, well-formed features? Is it his physique—solid, muscular, sensual? Is it the sound of his deep voice, his rich laugh?* Studying him, she could not find her answer, but for some unexplainable reason she was enchanted by him, totally under his spell. She felt almost desperate trying to understand the magic emanated by him, and a bit anguished and even a bit terrified.

Then she asked herself the most heartrending question of all. *Am I in love with you, Jeff Bannerman?* That one she didn't try to answer, for the mere question brought such an unease to surface, she almost groaned aloud. She certainly didn't need to ask herself questions like that one. Frantically she clutched her head and jerked her eyes from him.

Without a word passing between them, they entered her apartment and went straight up the stairs to her bedroom. That annoyed her. To think she wanted him so badly she couldn't even talk. Conversation was definitely out. Her physical self was ruling her, making her helpless and mute and terribly disillusioned with her own self. She felt like she should have, or he should have, at least said something, anything. Even something trivial would have sufficed. But not a word. Passion had made mutes of them both; desire had rendered them speechless.

Once they stepped into the room, he said thunderously loud, "Ooooh, this room smells like you do."

Shamelessly stripping from her dress, she stared at him.

Removing his shirt with quick movements, he laughed. "What is it, this fragrance—and I use the word for lack of any other."

She placed her dress on a hanger and said, "Jasmine, and something else—lust, I believe," she said coolly.

Sitting in the chair, he untied his shoes, looking at her and laughing softly under his breath. Then in a low, hoarse voice he said, "Come here, Kasha."

Thoroughly disgusted with her eagerness, she said, "What! I still have on my slip, and bra, and hose!" But even as she spoke she edged to where he sat in the chair with only his trousers on. "Jeff," she sighed, dismayed, "we're acting like two over-aged, over-sexed fools." They were, and she knew it, but still she moved into magnetic arms.

Smiling, he reached up and pulled her down onto his lap, his arms wrapping around her, embracing her in warmth. "I know," he agreed, a hidden laugh in his voice. "But we will get better in time." His lips burned into her shoulder.

When he raised his face to hers, he saw clear shining dark eyes looking at him questioningly. "I love you," he said in a whisper. "I don't want to disappoint you. If we're moving too fast, I'll slow down. I love you, Kasha, and I want to make you happy. I really do."

She laid her head on his shoulder. "I think I may love you too." She sighed forlornly.

Resting against her neck, his lips curved in a smile. "You do love me," he stated with sureness.

Her lips parted and she said with deliberate slowness, "You will not tell me what I feel."

His lips trembled against the soft flesh below her chin. "You're right, of course, I will not presume to decipher your feelings."

She straightened in his arms and her own went around his head, locking his face against the soft flesh above the lacy bra. His mouth opened and his breath was hot as his lips traveled a fiery path across her skin. His hands swept up her back and released the clasp, leaving her bare to his ravenous mouth.

She was flooded with warmth, near excruciating in degree, sweeping north and south and east and west, until no part of her was spared. His mouth, his tongue, made her shake as though she were being whipped by fire. With a small irrepressible cry, she caught his face with her hands and for a breathless instant looked into eyes of light blue enamel tinted with fire. Her mouth went swiftly to his, her fingers sliding back into thick soft hair. She kissed him softly, then fiercely, mouths opening and tongues lunging together hungrily.

His hidden tremors became little ripples across his back and her hands slid down, her fingers wide, flexing, wiping out the tremors, then making new ones surface. She tasted his moan, and when it was fading, her tongue evoked another.

In a purely frenzied state, he stood, bringing her up from the chair with him, holding her with arms of bronze. When her feet touched the floor beside the bed, her hands went out to his waist, her fingers sweeping the taut muscles of his stomach. Touching his hot skin sent a new chill of excitement through her.

When his trousers were on the floor she continued to explore him, allowing her hands to wander along the most sensitive area of his existence until his arms came around her shoulders possessively and he began eagerly to kiss her neck, her ears, her hair. When his mouth covered hers, her throat gave up an involuntary cry of delight.

She stepped backward and lowered herself onto the bed and he came with her. Slipping from around him, her arms fell out wide across the bed. He raised himself and his hands went slowly to her waist, clasping the slip and hose. In one graceful, sure movement he bared her.

Her fingers dug into her palms as his lips stung her toes, her ankles, and traveled up along her legs. She tried to look at him in the muted light of the bright moon that flooded the room, but her head drew back on the pillow and her lips closed against the resistance to keep them open.

His mouth and tongue flirted with her body, arousing near-maddening sensations until she felt disoriented and almost wild. His mouth was on her stomach, then he was covering her breasts again, kissing them softly, lingeringly, slowly, very slowly until she felt her heart would slam through her rib cage. Her lungs expanded and held, then she gasped aloud, a wail, a cry, "Jeff!" He had stretched her feelings, the tight sensations until she felt herself drowning in them.

His face appeared over her face, a hint of a smile curving his lips. For a moment he was completely motionless, his passion-filled eyes peering deeply into hers. He moistened his lips and said, "Kasha, do you have any idea how much I love you?"

She merely looked at him, feeling a surge of bewilderment fill her, but she thought, *If you think you're going to start plying me with questions now, you are badly mistaken.* Her arms went around his neck with lightning speed and she ground her mouth on his, her tongue moving ferociously over his, demanding his silence, erupting the passion he had so carefully maintained in a locked reservoir.

Her kiss broke the dam; he flooded her, he filled her. They kissed wildly, unrestrained, and her legs entwined with his while their bodies moved to a new cadence.

Her mind did not rest, though, as together they soared toward fulfillment. She still could not understand how this man's touch mysteriously changed her into a person she had not ever been. She didn't understand it, but she knew it was beautiful. She didn't understand the mystery of herself any more than she understood the man in her arms, for suddenly he became abruptly still and the echo of his hoarse, gasping words resounded in her mind, "Please say you love me."

Her eyes opened and she lay there for an endless time, then to her own surprise she whispered breathlessly, "I love you." And if she had said, Here is the key to King Solomon's mines, he could not have been more emotional, or tender, or gentle, or loving.

The possessive cadence came back, but with a difference, as if those three little words had magically pierced the last barrier separating them and made them one forever.

Trembling wildly in the circle of his arms, the deep hunger that had been a part of her life was suddenly satisfied and sensitively overflowing. They lay in each other's arms the longest time without a sound except the quickening breaths slowing and finally becoming deep and normal. Instinctively she knew she had freed that part of herself she had always kept hidden and untouched. Jeff had touched it and set it free and she was a bit frightened by it all.

Her fingers awoke and ran through the golden hair at his temples. Her heart felt strangely twisted and unsafe as she murmured, "Jeff, what are you thinking?"

He raised his head and smiled contentedly at her. "I was just thinking my first arithmetic teacher erred. One and one do not equal two, but rather, one and one equal—one." His fingers reached up and touched her hair at the side of her face. "You know," he continued softly in a near whisper, "that first time I saw you on the sidewalk outside your building, I felt something, kind of a tug inside I had never felt before. I was leaning against a palm tree talking to the foreman and I just casually glanced across the street and there you were. You had on a dark skirt with a slit in the front and a wisp of a breeze flattened one side to your leg. I watched you reach down with such poise and sweep the skirt back into place. Then you turned and went inside the building." He laughed softly. "I don't know till this day what the foreman said to me, but I remember nodding and saying 'Yes, sounds good.' From that day on I was a goner. I watched for you and every time I saw you I would feel the same tug—it was kind of a lost feeling—until I just couldn't stand it any longer. You made me a believer in love at first sight."

"Jeff," she whispered, a professional detachment slipping unconsciously into her voice, "what happened to your engagement?"

She suddenly felt him stiffen, but instead of answering he leaned over and kissed her mouth. Then he kissed her again and again—until she forgot the question.

## CHAPTER TWELVE

She remembered the question after he had left her apartment at five thirty the next morning. She remembered it while she bathed and packed for the weekend convention in New Orleans. Suddenly it mattered that he had not answered, even though it had not mattered earlier. She even felt a tinge of exasperation with herself that she had allowed him to dissuade her pursuance of the question by drowning her with a new wave of love.

She pursed her lips thoughtfully while she fastened her weekender. When she returned she would not again allow him to escape that particular question. For some unknown reason she could not convince herself that the broken engagement and his "love at first sight" could be totally disassociated from each other. And she certainly was not up to being a rebound love, not with him she wasn't.

Waiting for seven and Roman, another thought nagged at her. Jeff had not at any time during the night mentioned New Orleans or hinted that she should not accompany Roman to the convention. She had decided to discuss it rationally with him should the subject arise, but the subject had not been introduced from his mouth, and she did not feel she should be the one to begin the conversation. Obviously she was sorrier than Jeff was that she faced this weekend with Roman. He had left her apartment with a kiss and a smile and a soft, "See you Monday." It had been all she could do to keep from inquiring into his sudden change of heart, but she stifled that impulse along with several others. Sitting at the kitchen table she was profoundly puzzled by it all.

At hearing Roman's car in the back lot, she rose from the kitchen chair, retucked her blouse into her lightweight slacks, and lifted her matching jacket, folding it over the arm holding the weekender. She stepped out the kitchen door to see a grinning Roman coming up the walk, a bright gleam in his dark eyes.

"Ready?" he asked cheerily.

She smiled bleakly and nodded one time. On the way to his luxurious car, she glanced over to Jeff's drive. Her eyes widened to see his car was not there. Then it struck her, that is, of course, how he would handle a situation he found to be adverse to his liking. Just drive away until it was over. She could see him sulking in some pancake house because his "instant love" had gone off for the weekend with another man.

Climbing into the car, she sighed with dismay, sinking down into the plush velour seats. Why couldn't Jeff have just stayed at his home and understood her reasons, and trusted her judgment? That was why he hadn't brought up the subject during the passion-filled night. He simply couldn't deal with it.

She should have known and insisted on a discussion. But it probably would have turned out like the one on his engagement.

He was satisfied his own mother would not recognize him when he stepped up to the registration desk of the Carriage House on Bourbon Street in New Orleans. His thick blond hair was greased and parted high on one side, with long blond strands plastered to the side. The black-rimmed dime-store glasses were tinted and thick-lensed, with such magnifying power he had to peer out over the frames to see the young woman behind the counter. Above his top lip stuck a large sweeping, golden-brown moustache that had set him back forty dollars at the wig shop in Pensacola. His dad's large rust-colored sport coat didn't touch him anywhere but at the shoulders. He had been forced to wear his own trousers because the ones from his dad's closet had struck him mid-calf. Strangely enough, he found something stimulating about the disguise, maybe it was the thought it could become a deadly one if Kasha recognized him.

The young woman said, "Dr. Bennett?" the second time before his head jerked, realizing she was addressing him.

"Yes, I'm Dr. Bennett," he said, clearing his throat.

She looked at him with a quizzical slant of her head. "I know that, sir. You told me your name when you walked up. But what I asked is do you want to use a credit card?"

He shook his plastered head a quick time or two, then answered strongly, "No, cash. I never use credit cards—too easy to fall into the old credit-card-control-your-life syndrome." He smiled.

She stared at him in deadpan seriousness. "You're one of the psychiatrists, aren't you?"

He gave her a pleased grin. "How did you know?" he asked, placing two crisp one-hundred-dollar bills on the counter.

She shrugged, placing the money in the cash drawer and handing him back two ones, a quarter and a penny. "A little bird told me," she said half under her breath. Then much brighter, "We hope you enjoy your stay with us." Passing him the key, she gave him another smile.

He leaned forward slightly. "Now, this room is close to Dr. Lockridge as I requested when I called last week?"

Again she nodded. "Right across the hall, directly across."

Placing the key into his pocket, he turned back to the lobby, seating himself in a plush chair after placing his carryall beside it. Spreading out the newspaper, he settled back and yawned. Then he shook his head quickly. He couldn't afford to drop off to sleep. He would be able to tell from her appearance if that shrink jerk had given her a rough time on the trip over. And if he had, the Carriage House would soon be minus one prestigious guest, or maybe two. One would be in the hospital, the other, himself, would most likely be in jail. Then Kasha could enjoy this wonderful convention she had been so hell-bent on attending.

He shook his head slowly. Two hundred psychiatrists in a room together. He couldn't even imagine it.

Roman looked at her across the table in a coffee shop in Slidell, Louisiana. "Kasha, didn't you sleep well last night?"

She stared back at him through heavy lids, an innocent smile on her lips. "Why, yes, I did."

One side of his mouth twisted in a grimacing smile. "You realize I had to ask, considering you fell asleep three times in the middle of a conversation, and one time you even snored."

She maintained her innocent expression as she said, "I'm sorry, Roman, but riding in cars always makes me drowsy. However, I have never snored in my life."

He turned one side of his perfectly groomed dark head and peered at her dubiously. "Well, I hate to be the one to tell you, but that record is no longer intact. Coming through the tunnel at Mobile I thought we were being run down by a diesel truck. And I don't mind telling you that for a moment it frightened me. I have never been comfortable in a tunnel at best, and when you began snoring it did unnerve me."

She glared at him, her lips set in a firm line. She knew she didn't snore and she was not going to argue with him. However, he had provided her with a diversion in the drift of conversation. "When did you first realize your fear of tunnels, Roman?" she asked with as much interest as she could muster in her worn-out state.

He shrugged and thought a moment before answering. "The fear has been with me as far back as

165

I can remember. I think perhaps all the way back to my birth. My mother had an extremely difficult labor, my presentation was breech, therefore, I believe that the fear developed during the birth process when I didn't know if I would make it through the birth canal."

"Oh," she said, at the same time thinking, *How simple the cure, Roman. In the future just go through a tunnel butt first.* She sighed and looked down into the cup of coffee. Why had she not listened to Jeff just this one time? She was not yet to New Orleans and she had already been falsely accused of snoring and had been made aware of Roman's birth process. Shaking her head slightly, she drank her coffee.

An hour later, after Roman turned his large car down a one-way street, the wrong way, of course, and nearly scared her to death, they finally arrived at the hotel.

Hurrying inside with his hand at her back, he almost pushed her through the registration counter. His fear of missing the welcoming speech had heightened to near panic.

When the young lady behind the counter passed her back her credit card, she informed her casually, "Dr. Lockridge, Dr. Bennett has arrived."

Clutching her wallet and sliding the card back into the slot, she looked up suddenly. "Whom did you say?"

The young woman repeated with a buoyant smile. "Dr. Bennett, your colleague from Georgia."

Literally dragging her from the counter, Roman whispered, "Kasha, you didn't tell me you planned a reunion with an old colleague." He clutched her arm tightly, guiding her into the elevator, shaking his head at the bellhop trying to assist with the bags.

Once the door closed in the bellhop's face, Roman turned to her again. "Really, Kasha, I'll be very disappointed if you've made plans to share our time together with someone else. I don't think it was very fair of you."

She looked at him and said with simply dignity, "This may come as a shock to you, Roman, but I don't recall any Dr. Bennett."

He drew his chin in next to his throat and declared loudly, "You must. The man is here and inquiring about you. Obviously he knows you."

She stared thoughtfully a moment, then her eyes lighted. "Of course, Will Bennett, a classmate of mine in med school." She raised her brows in surprise and added, "But the last I heard of him he was doing a residence in proctology, which, of course, is at the opposite end of the spectrum from psychiatry."

Roman grunted. "Maybe he changed ends."

She shrugged. "I suppose it's possible."

Moving down the hallway to her room, she considered the possibility further that Will Bennett had changed specialties. On second thought, it wasn't possible. Not the Will Bennett she knew. Then she considered the possibility that Will just happened to be in New Orleans during this convention. That was possible.

But Roman did not allow time for additional considerations, for he called from his doorway, "We have ten minutes to get back down to the conference room."

"Don't wait for me. I'll meet you there. I've got to change clothes."

Once inside the room she felt her way to the soft double bed and collapsed in a dead heap. Then she turned over and sprawled out, glaring wearily at the ceiling. "Jeff," she said aloud, but weakly, "if I didn't have to show you that you are not going to rule my life and make my decisions for me, I wouldn't be here at this miserable moment. It's all your fault, and my dearest hope is wherever you are at this minute, you're as miserable as I am."

She slowly closed her eyes, envisioning him standing in the white sand in front of his magnificent little house and staring dully out over the Gulf waters. No, that would not make him as miserable as she. Relocating him in her thoughts, she put him inside his house, lying limp on his sofa with his Casablanca fans going full force, drinking beer and listening to Tammy Wynette. That worked, and with a smile curving her lips she pulled the spread up over her legs and fell into a sleep of exhaustion.

Jeff sprung up from the chair in the lobby, glaring wide-eyed at all the people gathered and milling around. How he could kick himself! He had sat right there in the lobby and gone to sleep. He had probably slept right through the most important time of his life. Then his gaze fastened on Roman Wells standing in the midst of a group, gesturing with one hand as he hogged the conversation.

His eyes scanned all the faces around, then rushed into the conference room where people were taking their seats. She wasn't there, not anywhere. Clasping his brow, he thought dully, *She didn't come. She changed her mind at the last minute.*

With legs of lead he went to the registration desk and asked the young lady, "Did Dr. Lockridge not check in yet?"

The girl smiled. "Yes, Dr. Bennett. About fifteen or twenty minutes ago."

He gestured with both hands. "Well, where is she?"

The young woman's eyes opened wide. "Sir, we just check our guests in and out, we don't keep up with them. However, I did tell Dr. Lockridge you had inquired about her."

His eyes blared behind the thick glasses. "You did!" He gave a little ill-at-ease laugh. "I'll bet she was surprised."

The young woman laughed softly. "She seemed less surprised than the man with her. He seemed very surprised."

Jeff nodded and grunted. "I'll bet."

With a low, almost inaudible moan, he went back to the chair and picked up his bag, wondering where she was. This was her big convention, the one she just had to attend, and she wasn't even attending.

Suddenly he straightened and hurried to the elevator. She must be in her room. If she wasn't anywhere else, she had to be in the room. But why? She was missing her convention. That didn't make sense.

Fast steps carried him down the hall and without conscious thought, he pounded heavily on the door directly across the hall from his own.

Slowly she roused her head from the pillow and

with much effort called out, "Okay, Roman, I'm almost ready."

Again he pounded.

Laboriously slowly she heaved herself from the bed and moved to the door. She started to speak, then put her eyes next to the peephole. Abruptly she sprang away from the door at seeing the malformed figure in thick glasses and bushy moustache. "You have the wrong room!" she exclaimed loudly, clutching her chest to slow the sudden onslaught of rapid heartbeats. It didn't take a psychiatrist to see a degenerate of some kind was outside her door.

On tiptoe she edged toward the phone. Without lifting the receiver, she waited for the pounding to come again. After a long interval of silence, she disengaged her hand from the receiver and tiptoed back to the door, biting her lower lip. She peered outside into the hallway. Sighing the longest breath of her life, she fell back against the wall. The man was gone.

She felt extremely annoyed with herself for panicking. The most reasonable consolation was the grotesque man had knocked on the wrong door. A simple mistake, and she had reacted like a Hitchcock heroine about to meet her doom.

After her heart slowed again to a normal pace she put the weekender on the bed and removed a two-piece business suit which she pressed before she quickly dressed.

It was amazing how a gallon of adrenaline dumped unexpectedly in the bloodstream could wake a person up. No longer the least bit sleepy, she slipped her feet into high heels, picked up her purse, and moved toward the door. Again she peeped out into the hallway.

The door opposite hers stood completely ajar and inside stood the culprit responsible for taking a good ten years off her life. The distance made him appear less frightening in appearance, but merely seeing him did not inspire the kind of confidence she needed to open the door.

Then he turned and she saw his profile. Her mouth parted with disbelief. It was Jeff. Jeff Bannerman had followed her to New Orleans! The panic she felt a few minutes earlier was nothing compared to the sudden rage she directed at him now.

She stood in motionless silence for the longest time, unable to produce a clear thought. She flushed, then paled as her mouth hardened. He didn't trust her. There could be no other explanation, and it was the worst possible thing that could happen to a relationship such as theirs. It depressed her to the point of tears.

Walking moodily back to the bed, she lowered herself and sat down. Her hands clamped together in her lap and her shoulders slumped. How could she have allowed herself to fall in love with someone who wasn't all together between the ears? She had blatantly disregarded every inner warning, and in doing so she now sat directly across from the outcome—a bushy moustache, black-rimmed glasses, and enough grease on his head to fry a chicken.

She sighed, feeling that she might never recover from this. If she didn't love the fool, there would be no problem. But she did love him. Where to go from here? That was the question, and there didn't appear to be a clear answer.

She wouldn't allow herself to feed his ego by ignoring the fact she knew it was him, nor did confronting him provide the answers she sought. She simply did not know what to do. In the back of her mind she kept repeating, *He doesn't trust me . . . doesn't trust me.*

Suddenly a thought began to lurk to the surface. Renewed strength gave substance to her plan. He didn't trust her now; she wondered how he would handle total betrayal?

On tiptoe she went to the door adjoining the two rooms and opened it. In near silence she changed rooms with Roman, and when it was done, she casually lifted her purse, went out the door opposite Jeff's, and twisted down the hall to the elevator.

Sitting in his room, Jeff felt absolutely rotten. His chin rested on his chest. Following his impulses without thinking through the complete situation was a fault he would soon have to correct. On a crazy impulse he was risking his entire future with the woman he loved. If she recognized him, she would never give him the opportunity to explain his actions. She would only see what he had done, and never know why, because she would not listen to his explanation. And thinking about it now the reason would be pretty flimsy. He was there to protect her against Roman Wells. He sighed long and heavy. Whatever made him think she needed protection? She had lived her life thus far without Jeff Bannerman's protection.

A strange somberness filled the room. Slowly he

172

got up from the chair and lifted his bag from the floor. He couldn't risk losing her over two words, *at last.* He was going home while he still had time.

A few minutes later, climbing into his car, he pulled off the moustache and the glasses, and with one hand ruffled his hair.

Pulling the car on to Bourbon Street, he felt an enormous relief. Some loves could be lost in a lifetime with full recovery possible, but some could not. The love he felt for her fell in the latter category.

Humming under his breath, he went up the ramp to Interstate Ten and sped toward home.

Throughout the afternoon sessions she sat next to Roman, twisting her hands. When she told him of the room exchange he had merely grinned and said, "Fine."

The presentations went on, but her concentration was everywhere except on the various speakers. She realized with each passing minute how devastated she was by Jeff's actions. She continuously threw glances back over her shoulder for a glimpse of him, expecting to see him appear in the back of the room at any time.

Finally, between speakers, Roman gripped her on the shoulder and whispered over, "Kasha, what are you doing?"

She looked at him with a start. "Oh, nothing."

His fingers tightened. "Why are you looking to the back of the room? Are you expecting someone?"

Her brows rose and she said coolly, "Oh, no, I was just checking the fire doors."

He turned his head back to the platform, saying

173

under his breath, "The fire exits are down this way." He nodded toward the front of the room.

She clutched her brow. Why didn't he just walk in? She could see him out in the lobby lurking behind the potted plants, or sliding down the hallways, or hovering in a corner peering out over the thick-lensed glasses. She hoped he realized the seriousness of driving someone in her profession bonkers.

At five thirty the session concluded and she leaped up from her chair and dashed out into the lobby, quickly scanning the area through narrowed eyes. If he was supposed to be spying on her, where was he!

Roman interrupted her search with the question, "Would you care to have a cocktail, Kasha? We have time before the banquet."

Wordlessly she accompanied Roman into the lounge. If anything would pull him out of the wood-work, this certainly would.

She ordered a glass of sherry and watched the doorway, expecting to see Jeff come storming through and physically remove the glass from her hand. When he didn't, she began feeling slightly exasperated.

By banquet time she was dazed. Not one glimpse of him. Throughout the meal strange little thoughts gnawed at her. Thoughts like, could she be one hundred percent, positively sure it had been Jeff she had seen in the room across from hers? She had not seen him up close, unless calling that malformed face on the other side of her door up close.

Roman looked over to her with an air of disgust. "Kasha," he said softly, "you've hardly touched this delicious meal, and you've not said a word to anyone

174

since this convention began. What *is* wrong with you?"

She turned and looked directly into his dismayed eyes, then said in her most professional voice, "You know, Roman, I may be cracking up." She nodded and lifted her dessert fork.

He merely stared at her for the longest time before turning his head back to face the speaker's table. From the corner of his mouth, he whispered, "Try not to create a scene here, Kasha. You'll be ruined forever if you do."

"All right," she replied dryly. "I'll just eat my dessert."

Following the banquet and the rambling speech that went on for a full hour and a half, Roman rose from the table and suggested, "Why don't you just go on up to the room and rest, Kasha. I'll stay down here and mingle for a while."

"Maybe I should." She sighed. "I am tired."

He smiled condescendingly, wrinkling his nose. "Do. I think you'll feel better in the morning."

Her eyes widened with surprise. "What about our late-night wine session?"

He gave an ill-at-ease laugh. "The doctor prescribes rest. I'll check with you in the morning."

She raised her brows and breathed, "Who am I to argue with the doctor. Good night, Roman."

Walking away from him, she casually approached the registration counter, turned, and sauntered a few steps before stopping and facing a young man alone on duty.

"Yes, ma'am?" he said.

"Tell me," she inquired, "is Dr. Bennett in Room 312?"

He eyed the register a moment before glancing up. "He was, ma'am, but it shows here he checked out a few minutes before noon."

Her mouth parted. "Are you sure?" she asked, not attempting to hide her astonishment.

He pulled his shoulders up slightly. "That's what it says here. He checked out at eleven forty-seven."

Stepping onto the elevator, all her thoughts went awry. Could he not do one single thing that made sense? If he was going to spy on her, what was he doing checking out of his room before noon? What spy would do something like that, leave himself without a safe harbor to return to when the going got rough?

Appalled by the latest discovery, she was more than a little puzzled. She was flabbergasted. If his intention was to destroy her brain, he had succeeded.

Stepping from the elevator, she looked up and down the corridor. Then she felt it deep inside. He was gone. Shaking her head, she sighed. Mercifully she refrained from tearing out her hair.


Near dusk Sunday afternoon Roman dropped her off at her condominium with a soft-spoken, "See you tomorrow, Kasha. And remember what I said about switching over to active practice. You see what continuous counseling of marital problems has done to you."

She smiled sweetly. "I'll think about it," she said, slamming the door.

Walking slowly up the walk, she glanced from the

corners of her eyes to his drive. His car was there. That meant he was close by. And that meant he was only seconds away from facing her.

# CHAPTER THIRTEEN

Upstairs in her bedroom Kasha changed into black shorts and zebra striped shirt. She wasn't an apprentice dealing with serious problems confronting relationships. All the pitfalls were clearly labeled in her mind, with there being none greater than overpossessiveness and jealousy. Even the strongest of affections crumbled when hurled against the barrier jealousy erected in the path of love. That barrier could not be vaulted over, or walked around. It was too high and too wide. It could only be removed, eliminated, for the relationship to survive and be healthy.

She loved Jeff Bannerman, she truly did, but she would let him go before she would continue with a relationship founded on quicksand.

Inhaling a long deep breath, she walked over to the window and looked down at the beach reflecting the soft colors of sunset. Low pink, silvery clouds floated out over the shiny Gulf water. She saw him sitting in the sand, leaned forward, his elbows resting on his knees. She stood beside her window and watched him for several minutes, contemplating his thoughts.

Then she took another deep shaky breath, walked

slowly down the stairs, went deliberately out the door, and moved along her path to the beach, her hands restlessly swinging at her sides.

Approaching him slowly from behind, she noticed the freshness in the air, became aware of her heightened susceptibility to his sensuousness. *So this is love,* she thought. How strange she had never before really understood this feeling that was so much a part of nature. It was much like being caught helplessly by some strong current much too powerful to swim against, and unsure of where it will sweep its victim if allowed to travel unprotested.

She walked up to him and stood a few feet from his side. He slowly turned his head up to look at her, and when he saw her, he smiled. "Hello," he said, hardly audible.

Without returning his greeting, she seated herself on the sand beside him, but not too close.

His stare fixed on her. "Have a good trip?"

She pursed her lips and looked at him. "Fine," she said in a quiet tone.

He nodded and lifted a handful of sand, then allowed it to drift slowly through his fingers. After the sand was gone, he stared at his empty hand and said, "I missed you."

After a pause, she answered, "Then why didn't you stay?"

His eyes widened as they sat facing each other for what seemed like forever before he said with a tinge of uncertainty, "You knew I was there?"

"Yes," she said forcefully, then repeated with emphasis, "Yes, I knew you were there."

He turned his eyes to the sand between his feet and

said without looking up, "I was a fool. I realized you didn't need me to look after you. You're quite capable of doing that yourself."

She suddenly blurted out, "Look after me? Jeff, what do you mean, look after me?"

He was silent, then looked unblinkingly at her. "That's what it means. I went down there to protect you from your partner. I overheard him in a restaurant earlier this week." He sighed heavily. "And the thought of you having to fight him off got to me, at least until I sat down in my hotel room and thought about it. And when I thought about it, I realized you didn't need me. So I checked out and came back."

She turned her head rigidly to her right shoulder and asked, "What exactly did you overhear?"

He blurted out, " 'At last.' That's what I heard. 'At last.' And the way he said it rattled something loose in my head."

She scanned the water at the horizon, her eyes narrowing. "And what do you think he meant by those words?"

Jeff reddened. "It's pretty obvious what he meant, Kasha. He would get you out of town, alone in a hotel with him. It was pretty obvious what his intentions were."

"What do you think happened?" she asked quietly.

His mouth turned upside down. "Nothing," he said in a sincere tone, then repeated with a single shake of his head. "Nothing."

There was a protracted silence, then she asked, "Why not? Why do you think nothing happened? You don't know, you left. How can you be sure?"

He glanced up at her. "Listen, Kasha, I didn't hurt anybody by going down there but me. I said I was a fool. What more do you want me to say? I went because I thought you might need my protection, and when I got there I realized you didn't. I came back—end of story."

"Not quite," she said matter-of-factly. "There's a little more to it than the neat package you've laid out, Jeff. It wasn't only that you feared he might try to overpower me, but you also feared I might allow it. You feared I might have too much to drink. You made excuses for me for why I needed your protection, not only from Roman, but from myself." She faced him directly. "You didn't trust me, Jeff. That's why you thought I needed your protection—from myself."

"If you had all the answers," he said roughly, "why did you bother to ask?"

She confronted him with the point-blank question. "What happened to your engagement?"

He turned his head so that she could see only the back of his head. He stared directly at the west when he said, "What happened to my engagement is totally unrelated to my being a fool this weekend."

"Is it?" she pursued quietly. "Or did she betray you?"

Slowly he rose to his feet and looked down at Kasha with an unfathomable expression on his face. "You could say she did," she said somberly. "She married my best friend, eloped with him while I was at sea." Walking away from her, he said quietly, "I suppose that's the ultimate betrayal."

She did not follow him. She couldn't. Frozen in a

layer of disbelief, she sat there on the sand until night fell on her, feeling a sensation of sickness deep in her stomach. But even knowing she had brought the past alive, she didn't regret it. She was sick about it, but she didn't regret it. It explained everything—his unorthodox actions, his rush to love, his possessiveness, his protectiveness. The closest people in the world to him had betrayed him—his best friend and the woman he loved.

She was rarely surprised, but Jeff's admission had surprised her. And yet, for some inexplicable reason she felt that she still did not know it all. There was something more than the words he had spoken. And instead of going on, he had walked away from her. Why?

Jumping to her feet, she rushed up the path leading to his house and knocked loudly on the door. When he pulled it open, she stepped back and looked at him. "May I come in?"

He leaned against the door and folded his arms. "I don't want you analyzing me, Kasha."

After a pause she asked flatly, "How about love, do you want me to love you? You said you did, but do you really?"

"You know I do."

She shook her head. "No, I don't. It's very easy to fall into bed and physically love someone, but I'm talking about a deeper love, not the physical love at all. Jeff, we are both guilty of playing games with each other, me as well as you, and I think it may well be that we're both afraid to commit our hearts. You indulge yourself with the pain of the past, and I indulge myself with the present with what I see and hear in my office daily. We're simply afraid, both of us. And at this point we need to eliminate the fear, or stop the game. If we continue on this way, we will have only the shallowest of loves—and it won't last. Believe me on that. Love has to be more than a physical game."

"Well," he said with a quiet smile, "why don't you come in and let's talk about it."

She followed him into his living room and sat down beside him on the sofa, pulling her legs up beneath her. She looked at him, seeing an expression of warmth on his handsome face, a tiny smile lingering at the corners of his mouth.

"Where do we go from here?" he asked softly.

She gazed at him engagingly. "Backwards . . ."

He moistened his lips. "I see." He inhaled deeply. "Do you want something to drink?"

She shook her head.

"Kasha," he began slowly, "it's not that I haven't told you because of what I feel, but rather I was concerned about how you might feel, what you might think."

Her expression didn't change. She was silent and he continued slowly. "I'm sure what happened with my engagement wasn't planned. It was just one of those situations where two people found themselves thrown together, at dances, dinners, various social gatherings. They fell in love, or rather they believed they fell in love. But neither had the fortitude to tell me, so they did the cowardly thing—they married, then told me. In the beginning I blamed the two of them. But I had a lot of time to think about it and after a while I shifted some of the blame to my shoulders. Emily wasn't an independent strong-willed woman like you, not at all." He suddenly frowned. "She didn't want the long engagement, but I insisted. I felt it would be a mistake to marry when the circumstances were such that I would be away so much of the time. We became engaged when I still had fourteen months to serve. We set the date the week following my release from active duty. I had my mind settled about the future. I knew I would be taking over the construction company. It's what I wanted to do; I'd been a part of it from the time I could go to the sites with my father as a child."

He shook his head. "Needless to say, I came home a trifle upset. For a month I didn't do anything except hide in my apartment and drink too much beer. Then one day my dad came storming in, yanked me around a bit, then told me something I'll never forget. He said, 'Son, worse things could have happened, she could have married you.'"

"Do you feel that way, Jeff?" she asked in a near whisper.

He smiled and gestured with one hand. "I didn't then, but it seems at some point in life you always face your past. I faced mine two months ago. She's divorced now, has a little boy of four, and she came to Pensacola to look me up. She wanted us to go back in time like the last six years never happened. And that's when I learned you must face the past, but you can't go back there because it doesn't exist anymore except in a memory."

He faced her directly. "And then I saw you and my attention became focused on the future, not what lay behind me."

She nodded. "And all this happened in about the same time period—her coming back, you seeing me?"

He grinned and his eyes crinkled. "Yes, Doctor, but I'm one step ahead of you. One had nothing to do with the other. I felt you would try and correlate the two events and that's why I haven't told you prior to now."

She glanced around the living room, then raised her brows questioningly at him. "How can you be sure, Jeff? I'm not at all certain that the two incidents are unrelated."

He chuckled. "See, what did I tell you?" he said assertively. "I knew you would do this, and there's not a thing I can say to keep you from doing it." He inhaled deeply, then sprawled across the sofa, placing his head in her lap. "So, analyze me."

She stared down into his face. The touch of his head against her abdomen, the feel of his hair crushed against her naked legs, distracted her immediate thoughts.

Then he said with laughter in his words, "But before you begin, I want to know if you were a happy little girl?" His sparkling eyes searched her face.

"For the most part," she murmured.

"And your teen years?" he whispered.

"I survived." Her face drew magnetically closer to his.

"And your past loves?" he said hoarsely.

"Past acquaintances," she corrected him, then added, "All are past." Her mouth lingered just above his, so near she could feel his breath warm on her lips.

"And your present love?"

"He's crazy," she whispered into his mouth. "And even worse, he's driven me crazy."

In a quick, sure movement, he caught her mouth firmly, then grazed her lips with a caress as soft as the foam sweeping the sand below them as he said, "He's willing to undergo lifelong analysis with you."

Tiny little waves of desire arose throughout her, charging her voice with emotional tremors. "It's much too soon to speak of lifelong commitments. We mustn't rush."

His eyes widened and he gazed up at her. "And when would be the acceptable time to speak of such commitments?" he asked in a hoarse voice.

She inhaled a long breath of determination. "In time."

Blue eyes searched hers and his fingers went up to her neck, touching her softly. "Now is time."

"But not time enough," she said with a little smile.

He looked baffled. "How long do you think it will take you?"

"At least until the end of summer. Jeff, I want us to be sure, really sure."

His head rose in genuine bewilderment. "I am sure. I love you, Kasha, and I'm sure I do. I'm also sure I will."

She looked into eyes of disappointment. "Then you won't mind giving us a little more time, will you?"

He thought a moment, then asked, "Could we start sharing all our meals? I think it's important to like someone you love over breakfast, don't you?"

She nodded thoughtfully. "Yes. But I eat a very light breakfast, usually just diet bars and coffee."

He sat up, his side pressing into hers, his arm draped around her shoulder. "That's not a problem; I'm a cereal person." He pursed his lips. "You know, we could pool our cars and ride into town together. We'd save gas and we wouldn't have to make that long drive alone. Do you think that's an acceptable idea?"

She eyed him with a glint of growing suspicion. "Yes, I think that's acceptable."

He inhaled deeply. "Well, I certainly think we should spend time together after work. I mean, we'll have been apart all day except for eating lunch together. What do you think? We'll share our evenings together, sometimes eat in, sometimes go out, see a movie, do different things. I like to bowl. Do you?"

"The only time I tried I dropped the bowling ball on my foot."

He chuckled. "I'll teach you how. And on the weekends we can either stay at home or plan trips. How does that sound?"

She twisted her lips thoughtfully. "It sounds like we'll get to know each other."

Raking his hand through one side of his hair, he looked at her and smiled. "I guess there might be some advantages with time. I don't think I'll mind the wait."

Her eyes narrowed at him. "You neglected one part of the day, or perhaps I should say—night. What are your plans concerning the nights?"

He shrugged innocently. "Oh, I didn't think it

would be fair if I made all the plans. Why don't you let what we do with the nights be your decision."

"Fine." She grinned victoriously at him. "I'll sleep at my home, and you'll sleep at yours. That way we'll have some time apart, for ourselves."

His hand flew to his chin. "Wait a minute," he said quickly. "Maybe we should reverse this arrangement. You decide our daytime activity and I'll take charge of the nights." He rubbed his jaw and looked at her imploringly. "Or maybe we should just take it a day at a time and decide together."

She stared at him, the slow grin widening on her lips. He wasn't hopeless, at least not totally hopeless.

"Now, that is certainly acceptable," she whispered. "We will make decisions concerning our lives —together. We have a good deal to learn about each other, and I'm very optimistic."

He leaned over and kissed her cheek. "Don't let that be known or you'll be kicked out of your profession. I've never heard of an optimistic psychiatrist."

Ignoring him, she said firmly, "And Jeff, one other thing, I have noticed you tend to be careless in your work. I don't want to look out my window and see you again on the sixth-floor beams without your safety gear on. If I'm going to love you, I don't want to walk out and see your remains on the sidewalk. If you fall, you won't fly—and that's a fact."

He gazed fixedly at her, then leaned over and kissed the other cheek. "Agreed. I'll be more safety-minded."

She flushed. "I want you to stop kissing me while we're laying out our groundwork. It interferes with my concentration."

Both hands went to the sides of her face and he brushed her lips before murmuring, "How does it interfere?"

The ever-increasing lightness in her head rose higher and she half-whispered, "I don't know exactly, it just does."

"Do you feel like there's a white flame inside you, burning brightly and blindingly?"

She placed her hands on his shoulders and shook her head, saying softly, "No, I would say more like a big wave."

His mouth closed over hers in a very long kiss. At that point she found herself no longer able to think clearly. It was madness; she was sure it was, but as that kiss became another and still another, she knew she preferred this madness to sanity. He was warm and alive, and she loved him so much she felt her heart would burst from the happiness of it.

Then he peered out at her from under long lashes and whispered against her lips, "It's night, time for our first decision together."

She laughed softly.

# Candlelight
# Ecstasy Romances™

$1.95 each

At your local bookstore or use this handy coupon for ordering:

**DELL BOOKS**                                                      B154B
P.O. BOX 1000. PINE BROOK. N.J. 07058-1000

Please send me the books I have checked above I am enclosing $_____ (please add 75c per copy to
cover postage and handling) Send check or money order   no cash or C.O.D.s  Please allow up to 8 weeks for
shipment

Name _____

Address _____

City _____ State Zip _____